AND THEN YOU WERE
GONE

Ivy Logan

notionpress.com

INDIA • SINGAPORE • MALAYSIA

ISBN 979-8-89556-848-4

Prologue

NINA

If only I could turn back time. My writing had the power to take you away from my life; why can't it exercise the power to return you? But I can't seem to bring you back. It's not that I haven't tried. Nothing works. You are gone, and you've stayed gone, no matter how much I wish it otherwise, or how much I try. My fingers tremble as they hover over the keyboard, my mind distracted by thoughts of you. If only I had been more careful, if only I hadn't interfered with your life, but however hard I try, nothing can change what happened. Each day I sit at my desk, desperately trying to find the words to bring you back to me. But do I dare? It's because of my writing that I lost you in the first place. I remember what happened the last time I took things into my own hand, the last time I thought I was helping. Perhaps had I not tried to help, you would still be here.

I am of two minds. I want to undo what I did, but I'm

terrified to try. Each time I put fingers to keyboard, my heart pounds in my chest, and the sound of blood rushes through my ears. What if I can't recreate the power that stripped you away from me? Worse, what if I do, but instead of making things better, I make them worse? I already have enough regrets to last me a lifetime.

My eyes glaze as I clutch the locket around my neck. It holds a picture of you and connects me to you somehow. I clasp it, tears streaming down my cheeks, the locket growing warm in my palm. The memory of you is so strong that it almost feels as though you are right there with me. I lay my head on the table, using my arm as a cushion. A feeling of helplessness envelopes me. I let you down when you were most vulnerable.

I didn't realize what I had done until it was too late. What was that quote again? *Act in haste and repent in leisure.* It looks like I have a lifetime of remorse waiting. I sigh, wringing my hands, staring at them with venom.

I lift my head, and my eyes fall on the photo frame by the window. Rising from my chair, I walk toward it. Instead of shuffling as they do nowadays, my feet seem to have purpose, a first in a long time. I gently lift the frame, the fingers of my other hand brushing away the dust accumulated on its surface. A tear plops onto the glass, and my vision blurs, but I ignore it, and soon, I can see your beautiful cherubic face—smiling victoriously because you are holding a ball in your hand. I treasure that memory.

My beautiful girl, now gone—what if it's forever? The

temporary dam I've erected crumbles, and I start sobbing again, clasping the photo to my chest, my head bowed in sorrow, my legs giving way until I'm kneeling on the wooden floor. My knees protest, but I welcome the discomfort, even though I know it will do nothing to ease the massive hole in my heart.

Then I remember I have something else of yours to hold on to. It's as though someone has lit a candle and shown me a path in the dark. I run—colliding with knick-knacks, tables, and other stuff, but I don't stop. Soon, I'm stumbling up the stairs. The need to know what happened is burning inside me, to see what your thoughts were. Understanding what you were going through might help me make things right. I curse myself for not thinking of this before. Finally, I enter your room ignoring the posters on the walls, looking down at me as if accusing me of invading your privacy. I don't care. My only lament is that I didn't think of this sooner.

One curtain is slightly open, so though the room is still dark, a little light streams in, and that is more than enough for me to make my way to the drawer under your desk. I yank it open, sighing in relief that it's unlocked, and my eyes shine triumphantly as I pull out your diaries—all of them pink and a few of them a little tattered but still a part of you. I hold one against my chest and close my eyes, trying hard to breathe in the lingering fragrance of your perfume. Time passes as I stay there, lost in a flood of my memories of you. I remember your excited voice as a seven-year-old when you told me that because your mama was an author, you wanted to keep a diary. You wanted to write like me and went through so many diaries over the years. Now, holding one of them, I know I am about to violate an un-written sacred mother-daughter code. Weren't diaries supposed to be private? But hadn't I already let you down? What was one more step down this path of self-loathing? I already hated myself for what I'd helped do to you.

I open its pages, and then it happens—your memories mingle with mine, and become one. You've jotted down all your thoughts, joys, fears, and every conversation you had, every one about you, every one you'd ever overheard. I'm now privy to them all. I'm taken back to the past as our lives flash before my eyes, but this time, I don't let the moments pass me by. Instead, I'm reliving each second through your memories and mine. I sit on the bed and go back to the day it all began. It's as though I am talking to you. It's as though you are by my side.

Part One

NINA

Dear Diary

I'm sad. The teacher asked us to write and read an essay on 'My Father.' The entire class completed their work except me. I didn't know what to write. Mama has never told me anything about my father. When the teacher asked me to read out what I had written to the class, I stood in front of everyone silently. Some kids laughed, but the teacher felt bad and asked me to return to my seat.

Mama is wonderful. Before going to bed, she gives me cocoa to drink, and after I brush my teeth, she reads her stories to me. She is a writer, you know. I love to listen to her stories. It is one of my favorite parts of the day. In the stories, we get lost in strange and mysterious places, and meet amazing people. She always says I can be the first to hear her stories, even before she writes them.

But she never tells me anything about my father. I wish I had one like the other children. I wouldn't feel so different.

CHAPTER 1
Nina

Sophie, I remember the day you were born sixteen years ago, like it was yesterday. My mind glosses over the pain, the blood, and the screams of childbirth, and all I recall is the moment I held you in my arms. I could forget the pain if I chose to. After all, our minds act like sieves, holding on to the memories we truly cherish and abandoning the rest. But I wanted to remember every second of the journey that brought you into my arms, even the unpleasant parts. You were so precious, and my chest felt like it would explode with pride. I stared at you in awe. All the feelings of maternal love that flowed through me in an undefined form before you were born were now focused and crystallized on you. I no longer felt lonely, and I knew with certainty that as long as you existed somewhere on this planet, I would never feel that way again. When I held you to my breast, you went at it like you had been trained in a premier 'baby school.' I looked up at the nurse and grinned. Her matter-of-fact, I've seen- this-a-zillion-times expression faded away as understanding flooded her eyes, and she smiled encouragingly.

Your dad was no longer a part of our lives, and I blamed myself. It was all my fault, but I wasn't sure how to feel about it. Was I holding on to him in a corner of my mind because I still loved or needed him, or was it merely a sense of obligation, an ode to a relationship that was never meant to be in the first place?

I met Tim on a visit to San Padre Island. I had been foolish, blowing up my hard-earned pay as a waitress on the fifty-dollar bus trip to the island, not to mention the entrance fee, telling myself I earned enough in tips to warrant this one-time luxury. While my friends were enjoying a surfing lesson, I opted to sit on the beach and watch the revelers, not wanting to spend any more money. People-watching was something I enjoyed doing, so why not? Several guys tried making eye contact, so it didn't surprise me when I looked up and saw a blond guy of average height, who seemed a little older than me, smiling at me. Nothing about him that made me wary, so I tentatively smiled back.

"Seat near you taken?" he asked.

I shook my head, a bit dazzled by his smile and crinkling hazel eyes. If he had been overly friendly or too pushy, I would have sent him packing, but I always had a problem dealing with polite people. I could never be rude to them.

"What are you thinking?" he asked me.

"Why should I tell you what I'm thinking?" Looks like I

was no longer having a problem being polite. Color crept up my cheeks. I never quite knew how to talk to guys. In a group, I was okay; I got by, but this… I was out of my depth. My friends always told me that if I continued with my rude replies when guys tried to chat me up, I would be single for life.

To his credit, he seemed unruffled by my prickly attitude. "I know I'm a stranger, but you seemed so lost that I wanted to know what you were thinking… I didn't mean to be intrusive. It just slipped out. Sometimes I talk without thinking." He smiled again. "I hope you get the irony of that?"

I gave him a pained smile. "Here is what I was thinking, and it's nothing special. I wished I was home with a book and you would leave me alone." I really couldn't help myself. Here was another insolent retort.

This time, I breached his defenses. He held his hands in front of his chest, palms facing me. "Woah! I will leave you alone. I'm sorry. I'm going."

His response calmed me down. I smiled. "It's okay. You can stay. I was just teasing you."

"You're sure?" He asked, his hesitancy obvious.

When I nodded, he laughed. "Do you like to read?"

"I do, and I think I like to write too." My confession surprised me and I bit my tongue. Why was I opening up to a stranger? First, I resented him for talking to me, and now I was confessing my innermost thoughts to him.

"Think!" he exclaimed. "You're not sure?"

"No. I am. I enjoy writing."

"But you haven't been doing any writing, have you?"

My mouth fell open. "How did you know that?"

"It was a wild guess. What's stopping you? If you want to write, you should."

Whenever I spoke about writing to the folks in my life, like my parents, they all had been pretty distant. They were wrapped up in each other and the sorrow of my brother's untimely death. While growing up, it often felt like I was a distraction and an outsider they could have done without. They ensured I got an education, but college never really cropped up. Frankly, there wasn't the money for it, and my grades were not the caliber to get me a scholarship. My parents washed their hands of me and assumed I'd find my way somehow. I didn't know what to tell this guy. If I enjoyed writing, why hadn't I written anything of substance? Folks don't always wait for someone to come forward and offer encouragement. They find time for stuff only they care about. Why hadn't I taken the plunge? What was stopping me?

"Have you done a writing course or anything?" His question intruded and further probed into my thoughts.

I shook my head. "Everything I know about writing is from the books I've read," I confessed.

I expected him to laugh or snort derisively, but he only smiled. "A reader's perspective is important for a writer. Understanding what a reader wants means you are half way to being a writer. So, don't lose hope."

This was the most encouraging anyone had been about my ambition to write. And I didn't even know his name.

As I turned back to stare at the ocean, he laughed. "I'm Tim." Was he reading my mind again? "Why did you get bored? Are your friends ignoring you?"

I stared at my sandals for a bit. I seemed to be making a habit of it while talking to this guy. "They are nice enough. They tried to get me to hang out but I realized I'd rather be alone."

"Why?"

"I haven't known them that long, and now I feel like I hardly have anything in common with them. I think I'm a bit of a loner. Coming here with them was an impromptu decision, I didn't give it much thought." I smiled sheepishly at him. "Also, I've realized I probably can't afford them." There I was, confessing things again. "I don't know why I'm telling you all this. We just met."

"It doesn't feel that way," he said, staring deep into my eyes, making me blush. "May I make an observation though?" He hesitated.

I nodded. What was he going to say? I could feel his trepidation, and it made me nervous.

"You don't seem very sure of yourself, do you? Everything you say is —I think, or I guess."

It was like he'd punched me right in my gut after being so sweet. I stared at him, astounded, and stammered, "You… you're incredibly ru…rude for someone I've just met."

His face colored. "As I said before, sometimes, I don't

know the right thing to say. I speak without thinking. I'm sorry. What I actually meant to say was that a lady as lovely as you should be more confident. I'm making an ass of myself, aren't I? I'm not able to explain myself properly. Look, give me a chance. Meet me once more. Let me make things right."

And on that injudicious note, my whirlwind courtship with Tim started. I reluctantly agreed to meet him when we realized we were both from Houston. One date turned into two, as he was on his best behavior after that first time. It appeared he learned how to think before talking, and he won me over. I admit I was in a fragile place with my confidence at an all-time low, and soon, he'd swept me off my feet. I don't think I made it very difficult for him. He felt like the perfect cure for all my troubles. When he decided to move from Houston to Austin, I impulsively decided to go with him.

"I want to do this right," said Tim.

"What do you mean?" I asked, swinging my feet from the wall where I was sitting.

"I don't want you to move unless we are married."

Was this a proposal? "You never came across as old-fashioned," I said, my voice filled with laughter, and just a bit of exasperation and shock.

"Here is an idea. Let's elope." Tim chuckled, and tugged at his shirt collar.

"I'm not saying no to the idea of being married, but what's the tearing hurry? Perhaps we could go down to Kentucky and visit my family. Spend time with them. Then, in the future, we could talk about marriage."

"Nina, I want to marry you. Just you and right away. I don't want to wait," he said, eyes shining. "Let's get married and then take things from there."

"Not in church?" I asked. "Is it that easy to get married?" Even to my ears, my voice sounded weak. Was this what I wanted from my relationship with Tim? Why did I feel like I wasn't ready? "Don't we need a license or something?"

"Come on, Nina. Let's do this. I have to move to Austin in two weeks."

"I can follow you, can't I? We can live together. We don't have to marry."

"Hmmm… the thing is… this company I'm moving to, they stress on family values, and I kind of told them you are my wife. I filed for a license weeks ago."

"What kind of company is this that you had to tell them you were married?" My jaw dropped. I couldn't help myself. All of this was getting to be too much. "You filed for a license weeks ago without asking me? But it's only been three months since we met."

"What's the difference between married and soon to-be-married? I knew you were the girl for me the minute I saw you on that beach."

His gallant speech mollified me a bit, but not that much. "But shouldn't we get to know each other better?" I buried my face in my hands. I was starting to feel dizzy. "You didn't even ask me."

"I'm asking now." He looked at me with puppy eyes. "Don't you know me? Why wait? You know you want to marry me. I'm eager to start our lives together. Come on Nina, say yes."

In a way, it felt like if I disagreed, I would lose Tim forever, and I didn't want that. I wasn't ready to lose him, so I said yes, and in four days, I found myself married. I couldn't help wondering if I married a guy who married me because he needed a wife. *He wants you for you,* I tried to tell myself. Should I have run and never stopped running until I got away? Perhaps. Instead, I ran straight into his arms. I decided my destiny lay with Tim. I was never a person who believed in myself, and seeing Tim's belief in me helped me fall in love with him and made me decide he was the one for me.

Married life suited me and Austin was right for me, though I couldn't shake off the feeling that a detail was missing. Tim was the model husband, attentive, caring and loving. He'd go to work, and I'd stay at home working hard to make our house into a home. I was happy but this was not how I imagined my life would turn out. I kept reminding him it was time for me to look for a job, but instead, he had me gobsmacked. "Why don't you write?"

"I can work and write," I insisted.

"How many pages did you write when you were waitressing in Houston?"

I shifted in my seat. "That was because…" I waved my hands in the air helplessly. I had no excuse.

"That's exactly what I'm telling you. You need this. This is what you wanted to do."

I wanted to write. But was Tim backing me because it suited him or because he wanted to support me? I shook my head. Tim was being so generous. Why was my perception colored? I should be happy.

I started writing and hoped it would make the unsettled feeling I was experiencing disappear. But it didn't. I kept telling myself I was okay. Once, after a long writing spell, I tried to get Tim to read my manuscript. That's when I got my first shock.

"What's this? I thought you'd use your time better," he said, shuffling through the pages. "I've been so generous by allowing you to write."

"Allowing me to write?" My tone was sharp. I couldn't help it. I was deeply wounded. "And you barely read it."

He smiled at me reassuringly. "I read enough. I'm only trying to help you. Perhaps it makes sense to you, but it doesn't to me." But then he spoiled it all by smirking. "I didn't know you were a fantasy writer."

Maybe Tim was right. My writing couldn't be everybody's cup of tea. But at least I was writing. That was the important thing. But that was the first and the last time I shared my writing with him. I couldn't bear to be humiliated again.

If that were the only problem, it would have been easy to forget, but that wasn't all. Soon, cracks I couldn't miss began to appear in our relationship. Tim forgot my birthday, our anniversary. Don't most men forget, you might say? But when I tried to celebrate these occasions, he seemed surprised. He asked me what was there to celebrate. This hurt a lot. It looked a lot like he had started taking our relationship for granted. He was always out late. Working, he said. I wouldn't have minded that. I really wouldn't. But then, why did he reek of perfume when he got home? I had to stop myself from questioning him. I think I already knew that our relationship had become so shaky that it wouldn't survive even a single bout of questioning from my end. So, I continued to play the docile housewife. But inside I was dying a slow death. Then, out of the blue, there would be days when he was so absurdly sweet and caring that I convinced myself the late nights and the perfume were manifestations of my imagination. I tried to bury these memories somewhere deep where I could forget, but then my anxiety would fester and sink its claws, unearthing those ugly reminders of Tim's faithless behavior and bringing out the worst of my fears.

I wanted to be happy, but I didn't want to be an igno-ramus fool, at least more than I'd already been. Because my mom and dad had been together for thirty-two years, and were still going strong, I tolerated a lot. Despite our difficul-ties, I hoped it would be the same for Tim and me. I was too ashamed to admit, even to myself, that I had failed. My marriage was going nowhere. I wanted to continue the charade for as long as possible.

The beginning of the end came when Tim announced he had an important sales conference to attend close to my due date. But perhaps the conference had only been the final nail in an already festering relationship. Occasionally I have the habit of seeing only what I want. You've pointed it out to me on various occasions. Perhaps that's my Achilles heel, besides loving you more than anything.

"You can hardly expect them to plan the conference around your pregnancy?" Tim said, shrugging his slim shoulders. "You were always the logical one. Why are you sounding like a hopeless romantic? What happened to you? You are not the woman I married. You're so needy it makes me sick."

He was right, but I couldn't stop thinking, *he won't be there when our baby is born.* Despite his rudeness, I could have smiled and let it go. But I did not. Was I being excessively needy? I think not. I just wanted him to be there for you, to welcome you into the world. As a baby, you wouldn't know if your dad was present at your birth or not. It wouldn't matter to you then but how about later? I was already your self-appointed champion, willing to fight every battle on your behalf until you were equipped to handle them on your own, and perhaps even then. "Hopeless romantic?" I snapped. "I only want you to be there when our baby is born." My lower lip quivered. I pressed my fists against my eyes and my lip jutted out.

"Don't pout." Tim wagged a finger at me.

"Our baby is coming. Doesn't she take precedence?" I stood staring at him, my fingertips pressing against my temples.

His expression turned stony. He looked like I had asked him to cross the Niagara Falls on a tightrope. "I told you I need to focus on my career. I wasn't in a hurry to become a dad. In fact, I wasn't even sure I wanted a baby." He pointed a finger at me again as I stared at him over my large belly, my mouth hanging open. "You did this. You deal with it."

"Got pregnant? It takes two, you know." I gritting my teeth. "And why do you get to decide everything—when we get married, or have a baby? Aren't I part of this marriage? Don't I get a say?" My voice turned conciliatory. "Just you see, a baby will make things better between us. She will bring us together."

He scoffed.

"If that's how you feel," I said, my shoulders stiffening, "go on to that conference." I put my hands on my hips. "But if you do, don't bother coming back."

I don't know what I was thinking. Perhaps I thought our marriage was stronger than it was? Maybe I was living in a dream world. But my pride had subdued my reasoning, and as I stared at him after issuing the ultimatum, I waited for him to crumble and give in, to grovel for forgiveness. Any moment now, he'd say, *forget the conference. You are more important, and our baby needs me.*

His lip curled into a sneer as he eyed me from head to

toe, taking in my shorts and the tank top straining over my stomach. "You, stupid cow. Deal with this yourself. I'm out." He turned and rushed into the bedroom where I could hear him shoving things into a bag. Then, he was out of the door as I sat there, my mouth hanging open again, my eyes widening when I realized what had happened. I'd given Tim an out, and he'd gladly grabbed at it.

"Come back here!" I rushed to the door, pulling it open, but there was only silence beyond the corridor. He was gone.

He will be back, I told myself. *And he will be sorry. He loves me. He has to come back.* But as the haze outside the window started taking on a purplish hue, and the birds fell silent, as I sat unmoving in the rocking chair, my eyes fixed on the door, I realized he wouldn't return. Your dad had walked out on us, and you weren't even born. What kind of welcome were you going to receive, little one, from a single mother with no relatives nearby and no visible means of supporting you? I didn't want to rush to my parents for help. I didn't want them to know I'd failed to have a marriage like theirs. They had enough sorrow to deal with. I didn't want to become another burden for them. My face crumpled. You were my ray of sunshine, a rainbow in a world that was fast losing color. I couldn't let you down. What were we going to do?

Tim taught me a lesson—love is what you make of it. The love between Tim and me had been toxic. One honed out of temporary attraction and long-term dependence. There was no symbiosis. I depended on him; I needed him to need me, and he encouraged that. Let's say he thrived on it. And when you came, and he was no longer the center of my world, he resented you for taking his place. He wanted the focus on him and his needs 24-7. The minute I started asserting myself and what I wanted from our lives together he was gone, without a backward glance.

I finally pushed up from my chair and hurried to the bathroom because my bladder felt like it was about to burst. Then I crawled under the blankets and tried to sleep, but pangs of hunger gnawed at my stomach. "Can't you cooperate for once?" I yelled. Almost immediately, I was repentant and regretted my outburst. I stroked my stomach, whispering, "I'm sorry. I'm sorry." My body and you, little one, were making your needs known. I had no reason to be angry.

Oh, I had cause to be upset with your good-for-nothing father and the world, but not you. I sighed and finally started making a sandwich, shoving whatever I could into it, in addition to the bacon and eggs I got going—the remains of some salad and even some leftover pasta. I started giggling, imagining Tim's reaction if he saw my non-conforming sandwich. My eyes glistened while I laughed. Then, I spooned the food into my mouth until my hunger finally satiated. But that's when all the doubts and fears came rushing back. I had merely pushed them into the recesses of my mind for a while to help me regain a semblance of control. But now, the doubts assailed me in full force. What was I going to do? I had a baby coming.

Lost in thought, I almost missed the peals of the telephone. Was Tim calling to say he was sorry? I rushed to answer, stubbing my toe against the dining table in my haste.

"Ouch. Hello?"

"Nina, what an exciting way to greet your caller," the voice at the other end drawled.

Disappointment flooded my veins. It was my agent, who I had signed up with just days before I found out I was expecting. "Beth, please don't make jokes. I'm not in the mood. Why were you calling?" An immense weight was bearing down on me. It felt as though I had mud running through my veins. *He didn't call. He wasn't coming back.*

"Why do you sound like you've been exercising? Jogging in your condition?" She laughed.

"Why are you calling?" I asked, barely able to hold back the tears.

"Nina, you don't sound like yourself at all." Beth's tone changed. She now sounded worried. She would be, as she was such a good person. I had been ill-mannered to her, but she would still be kind to me.

I didn't answer, holding onto the phone silently, with dramatic thoughts about Tim running through my head. *Why did I have to challenge him? Why couldn't I have kept quiet?*

Oblivious to the turmoil I was in, Beth was still talking. "This isn't how I expected this conversation to go, but here is the news. Realm Publishers loved your book. They want to sign you. Hello… Nina? Why don't you say something? Can't you hear me? You know what, I'll come over. Oh, and one more thing."

"What?" I mumbled finally.

"They are willing to sign a three-book deal with you. Can you do it? The advance will make your toes curl."

"Can I do it?" I laughed hysterically. "Of course I can. My life, our life" —I stroked my belly— "depends on it."

"Is something wrong?" I guess this desperate response wasn't the one Beth was expecting. She probably thought I'd sound more euphoric. "Did Tim say something, again?" I could sense the hesitation in her voice. Tim had once openly accused her of poisoning my mind against him, and I could understand her caution.

"No, Tim didn't say anything." I hung my head. *I'm the one who said everything.*

"That's good. That guy upsets you." Then it burst out of her. "Why don't you leave him?"

"I can't."

The next moment she was regretful. "I'm sorry, Nina. I know he means a lot to you, and you take your marriage very seriously."

As the words finally escaped me, I couldn't recognize my voice. "I can't leave him because he left me today, as it happens. Tim is smarter than me. He knew a sinking ship when he saw one. He didn't care about the baby, and he didn't care about me. He just walked out, and I know he is never coming back."

"Oh, honey." Her voice was full of sympathy. If she were in front of me, I'd be in her arms by now, sobbing my heart out. But I was alone, and the tears had dried up. I didn't realize she was still talking, trying hard to prop me up. "Nina, I know you're upset, but there is no reason to be so hard on yourself. If you left him, he would have guilt-tripped you into returning. This way, you can start with a clean slate."

"I never wanted to leave Tim. He was my safe-haven," I cried out.

Her tone sharpened and I could feel her anger emitting in waves. "He was anything but. He was an egoistic fiend who only cared for himself, and you let him get away with it for too long. You will get through this. And one day, you will look back and be proud of yourself."

"You mean it?" I wiped my dripping nose.

"I'm sorry for blathering on about the book deal."

"Why? It's huge. Isn't it just what I need right now?" I said, trying to sound happy. "You're the best agent ever and an even better friend."

"Despite my jokes?"

"Despite your jokes," I assured her, choking back a laugh. "See, you even made me laugh today when all I thought I would do was cry."

Dear Diary

Beth comes over often. Mama and she talk about books, but sometimes they also talk about how they almost didn't meet, how Mama nearly didn't become an author. I'm so glad they met. Writing makes Mama very happy. In addition to Nick's mom, Beth is one of Mama's best friends. I know she says she can talk to me about anything, but that's not true. She never talks to me about my father or her family. My teacher says it is important to talk about our feelings. But all Mama talks about to me is 'me.' What about her? I wonder if she talks to Beth about her feelings and about my father.

Nina

I think back to when I signed with Beth. It almost hadn't happened. Tim's pessimism and dismissal of my manuscript when I finally built up the courage to show it to him affected me. I remember sitting in the coffee shop, waiting for Beth. I was such a bundle of nerves; my knee jiggled up and down, taking on a life of its own, and my eyes kept darting toward the entrance each time the door opened. It was already March and giving a nod to the last dregs of the mild Austin winter, I was wearing a short-sleeved red dress with my denim jacket slung over the chair and cowboy boots with a thin pair of socks. I was of two minds. Did I even want the agent to show up? I wasn't sure. My nerves were getting to me. My body and my mind were at odds. I jumped up, my hand jerked out to grab my manuscript, and I spilled hazelnut coffee all over my dress. I stared in relief at the manuscript that escaped unscathed. But as I inhaled the earthy, nutty aroma of the coffee coating my dress, the server gaped at me, horror-struck at the mess she would have to clear up.

"I'm sorry, so sorry." I grabbed a couple of tissues in both hands and started swiping the table clean while simultaneously trying to salvage my outfit. Both ended up looking worse.

"Leave it," the girl said frostily. Relieved, I threw the wad of soggy tissues on the table, eliciting a frown from her, and I fled. As I ran out the door, I collided with a blonde wearing giant sunglasses that almost covered her entire face.

"Ahhh," she yelled as she fell back against the door.

I grabbed her shoulders and righted her, but my apology drowned in my throat as I saw the look of concern in her eyes. "Lady in red, why do you look like you're about to cry? Did someone hurt you?" Her voice was barely above a whisper.

I looked down, grimacing at my red outfit chosen with such anticipation, and shook my head as a sob escaped. "I'm a fool. What was I thinking? I'm sorry I slammed into you."

"No harm no foul." As she bent down to retrieve something from the ground, I took advantage of her distraction and made my escape.

"Wait ..." she called after me, but I didn't stop. I needed to get home and under the bedcovers where I would be safe and sound from the world. My bed and blanket were often the only thing between me and the turmoil in my life. Sounds silly, I know. But when I was under my blanket, even in peak summer, it felt like nothing could hurt me. Besides, it was still almost winter in Austin, so I had a good excuse.

I left so hurriedly that I didn't realize the lady was trying to return my manuscript or that she was the very person I was supposed to meet that day, Beth—the agent.

Reaching home and discovering I'd lost my manuscript brought a fresh bounty of tears. When Beth called the next day, I stammered out an apology. "I was ill. I'm sorry I couldn't show up. The thing is, there is no point in meeting because I looked at my manuscript, and I realized… it's… far from ready. I'm sorry I wasted your time."

"You apologize a lot." Her tone was curt.

"A lot?" This was barely the second time I'd spoken to her, and we'd never met.

"Tell me, how could you look at your manuscript when 'Deadly Love' is with me? I saw the note you put inside that takes great pain to emphasize this is your only copy."

"I have a soft copy," I murmured. What was she talking about? My hard copy had reached her—the woman I was dying to show it to? What kind of miracle was this?

"Lady in red, don't you remember me?"

Her voice was soothing, but the words sounded so familiar. When had someone called me— 'Lady in red?' Then I remembered—the café.

"You're the woman at the door I collided with?"

"You remember. Good. So, stop with your equivocating and tell me when can we meet?"

"You want to meet me?" I asked. "After my dismal behavior. What must you think of me?"

"It told me that you are an emotional person and that shows that you must be a talented writer, right?" Her laughter lifted my spirits before her tone turned serious. "We all have days when things don't go so well. Do we ever know anyone or understand what they are going through? Who am I to judge you? But I know your book, and I loved it! I hope you don't mind, but I read it, and through your writing, I saw your heart. Christian is a character to die for, and Bella is amazing. This book deserves its place in the sun, and I want to be the one to put it there. Your story is raw; the plot is intricate plot and unique from the usual shifter stories that come to my desk."

"I don't know what to say... my husband said... it was juvenile." I trembled at the unexpected praise. Living with Tim had left my self-confidence in shreds, and let's be frank, I wasn't a very confident person to begin with. I didn't know what to say to Beth. But it was okay because she seemed to do enough talking for the both of us.

"Juvenile? He isn't much of a reader, is he? And if he is, he is probably one of those pretentious people who only reads highbrow books."

"Well, yes. I think he likes to brag about what he is reading more than the reading itself."

Beth laughed. "Your writing has something for everyone."

"That's my purpose." My heart did a little somersault. *She got me. She did.*

Her tone turned business-like again. "I have a question for you. Is this a series?"

"It could be," I said, the stubborn writer in me fighting against the pessimist. I couldn't contain my enthusiasm. It was bubbling over. "Their story ended on a bit of a cliffhanger. I know readers don't like cliffhangers, but I resolved the storyline of book one and then hinted there was more to come. So…"

"It could be a series," she said, finishing my sentence. "I think this book will soon find a home." And that's how I suddenly went from un-agented to agented. From that moment, Beth became relentless in her search for a publisher.

And now she had come through for me. Was this really happening? Could things be turning around at the very moment I believed my world had gone dark? As I sank into my rocking chair, my hand over my heart, trying to tamp my excitement, you kicked my stomach, and my excitement levels shot up as though it was the first time. "Ouch! Sophie, are you happy for me? What? No, I didn't forget about you. I'm so happy. We are going to be okay. Can you hear your mama? We will be fine." I continued rubbing my stomach as I talked to you softly, letting go of Tim for the first time that evening.

Dear Diary

SOPHIE AGE 7

Mama often tells me stories of my time as a baby. She makes it sound like I was the best baby in the world. But I don't know. I sound pretty boring. Mama tells me our house was my palace of adventure, and the first challenge I took upon myself as a two-year-old was the baby gate at the bottom of the stairs. She sounds so proud. She told me I was eager to explore the rooms upstairs, and one loose spring on the baby gate couldn't stop me.

Mama goes on and on about my 'achievements' as a baby. She calls them milestones. I'm her only daughter. What else can she do but praise me?

I wonder what it would be like if my father had been a part of our lives? Would he have praised me too? Would his eyes shine when talking about me like Mama's do? Would he and Mama hold hands and gaze at me with pride and adoration?

CHAPTER 3
Nina

I know it's a cliché to say I fell in love the moment I laid my eyes on you, but it's true, yet so inadequate at the same time. Because I fell in love with you even before they put you in my arms. I fell in love with you when I realized I was no longer alone. You became the most important and exquisite part of me. There wasn't much that was beautiful in my relationship with Tim, but there was you. You changed everything for me. With you, my world was complete. I needed no one else.

Many new mothers complain about lack of sleep and having no time for themselves. Perhaps their old lives before the baby were so much easier. I envy them. But my old life was the one with Tim. I remember he came home from work one day, and I was on the phone with Beth.

He hated me talking to her, and I didn't want to start a fight. "I got to go. Tim's home."

Tim's eyes bored into mine. "Why do you keep yacking with that woman all the time? I told you she's a bad influence. She's putting all kinds of ideas in your head."

"Like what?" I furrowed my brow, not understanding what he meant.

"That you are an awesome talent. You're a housewife with nothing to do who has convinced herself she is a newly found star writer on the cusp of success. Wake up."

His words hurt so much that I could barely speak. "Th… th… that's harsh. You were the one who told me I could be a writer. You told me to believe in myself." Anger took hold of me. "Every time I find a job, you disparage it and say I'm better off at home. If I had a job, I'd contribute to our income too."

"Are you saying I don't earn enough?" He glowered at me.

I decided backtracking was the best option. "I didn't say that."

"Then shut up." He yawned. "Is dinner ready?"

I tried to sound cheery. "It's in the oven."

"What are we having?"

"Broccoli chicken casserole."

He grimaced. "I hate broccoli."

"Yesterday you said …"

"Oh, shut up. Stop blathering about what I said yesterday. I'm going out. I will be back late. Enjoy your casserole."

Every moment I spent with Tim had been a battle, each of us striving for victory, with me losing every time. But that's not what a marriage is supposed to be— a battle of wills. Had I been blind? Was he the same guy who swept me off my feet with flowers, poems and dinners? The same man who told me I would be a wonderful writer and that I was the next big thing waiting to happen? Why didn't I walk away? I think I started believing that I was nothing without him, that I wouldn't be able to find a job, and I would have no one to love and take care of and no one to take care of me; I would shrivel up and die.

It wasn't like that with you at all. You never made me feel inferior. You made me want to do more. To be the best version of myself. My love for you convinced me that I was invincible, and could do anything and everything for you. Perhaps that's where I went wrong. I was only human and meddling with things I had no business with ruined our lives.

But I digress.

My heart overflowed with love for you and when you looked at me with Tim's hazel eyes so similar, yet so different, I knew you loved me, too. During the early months of your life, you were content to sleep for long hours, allowing me to write. And before I knew it, I completed the second book in the series, '*Deadly Lives*,' for Beth.

I marveled at her trust in me. Not once did she insist I send her pages. Instead, she seemed satisfied to allow me to finish the book before she saw it. With your sleeping schedule running like clockwork, I had more than enough time to write. Wrapping almost eight hundred words daily, I had book two ready in no time.

You were a lovely baby. And I was so proud of you. When you were four months old, you snatched a rattle from my hand and shook it as though saying *come hell or high water, let's start this party.* I leaped up and started a little dance of my own, oblivious to the fact that you were busy with your new plaything and couldn't care less if it was a party of one or two. When you started crawling at ten months, I thought I had baby-proofed the entire house, but you kept showing me things I missed. We had a few narrow mishaps there. The thing I loved best was when we had food fights. You would put your hand into the bowl of mashed carrots and then squash it on my face, watching my expression with glee. *My baby is so smart*, I thought with pride, swiping the carrot with my hand and licking it from my fingers. We gradually started having little conversations. I would tell you about my plan for the day, and you would babble in your mysterious way, offering advice and baby wisdom.

Was I an over-protective mother? Perhaps, but then I had no one else but you. You were the culmination of everything good in my life, and best of all, you gave me hope for the future.

Dear Diary

SOPHIE AGE 7

Mama says she misses me when I'm at school. But now she is used to it. She says she found it very difficult to be separated from me when I was in preschool.

I don't have specific memories of my time in preschool. But I think we had a lot of fun. I kind of remember my teacher. She was real pretty, with curly black hair and light brown skin. I remember her skin was very smooth, and I liked to touch her cheeks. She used to gently pinch mine when I did and whisper, "Chubby cheeks, teacher's pet!" I think I was her favorite. Mama says her name was Gail.

Preschool was also where I met my best friend, Nick. Mama told me that on the first day, I advised Nick not to cry. He must have thought I was weird.

After school in the evening, Nick's mom and mine would take us to the park.

I remember falling one day. It hurt really bad, but I didn't want to cry in front of Nick. So, I sat on the ground, holding my tears back until Mama picked me up.

Nick kept saying, "Don't cry." But I wasn't crying. Couldn't he see that? Maybe he had sand in his eyes.

CHAPTER 4

Nina

I remember the first time I said goodbye to you. My anxiety skyrocketed, and I lamented the fact that we had never been apart, and now I expected to go a full three hours without you. The beautiful building with pillars designed in the shape of number and alphabet blocks and its lovely blue roof of slate shingles did nothing to ease my disquiet. I was there almost thirty minutes early to pick you up from preschool.

"Hi, my name is Sarah."

Another anxious mother, probably. She was early too. I had been woolgathering and stared at her blankly.

"I'm sorry to have startled you." The woman gave a nervous laugh as she started to back away.

Where were my manners? "Hi, Sarah, nice to meet you. It's not your fault. My head is in the clouds sometimes." I smiled at her as graciously as I could. "My name is Nina."

"Daughter or son?" she said.

"Daughter. Sophie. This is her picture." I proudly showed her a picture I always carried of you in my purse.

"Ah, I see the resemblance. The same ebony hair and green eyes."

"Hers are hazel." I smiled politely. The color of your eyes would always be a thorn in my side. Just a slight difference, and there you were—a constant reminder that you were also Tim's daughter.

She stared at me non-plussed, shrugging her shoulders. "Pfft. Minor difference."

My smile stretched a bit more. It was quite an effort. "Big difference. Every time I look at my daughter, it's like I'm looking into her father's eyes."

"Oh."

Foot in the mouth again. "That was too much information. Sorry," I said with a rueful smile.

"Are you finding it difficult to let go?" she said, her eyes, gentle.

"What? No. I'm perfectly fine. I'm worried about Sophie since today is her first day. I'm sure she must have bawled her head off without me."

Sarah gave me a lopsided grin. "I meant, your relationship with your husband."

"Oh! Not at all." I grimaced. "I've moved on. Not as quickly as he did, but I'm okay now."

"I see." I think she saw more than I intended to show her, and I felt a bit upset at the way my I'm-ok-I'm-fine mask had fallen away in front of this woman. She patted my shoulder, her eyes warm. "And don't worry, your daughter will be perfectly fine without you."

Why did I disagree with everything this woman said? The stubborn expression on my face must have told her how I felt. Sarah started to say a few words, but the door opened, and the teacher stepped out. Mums and dads, waiting to collect their children, were lining up behind me. The teacher looked at me questioningly.

"I'm Sophie's mom. She is the little one with—"

The teacher gave me a broad smile. "I can tell; you look so much alike."

"You know her?"

"I do. A lovely little girl."

"Sophie's eyes are hazel not green," said Sarah helpfully from behind me, as though trying to avert a disaster with the teacher too.

"What?" the teacher gave us a puzzled look. "Are you both related to Sophie?"

I shook my head. "I'm Sophie's mother. Sarah is here to pick up her kid. She is a new friend."

"A very good friend, it seems," said the teacher in a business-like tone, frowning at Sarah.

"Did Sophie cry?" I asked the teacher, trying to get the focus back on you.

"Not at all. You will be happy to know she was an absolute doll. She adjusted beautifully. She told a little boy not to cry, saying his mom would be waiting for him after school."

The teacher missed my shocked expression as Sarah piped in, rolling her eyes, "Her daughter can speak sentences?"

I opened my mouth to answer, but the 'in-house Sophie expert' was ready with an answer. "Almost." The teacher smiled, waving her arms. "I think Sophie's mom talks to her a lot, so her communication skills are excellent."

Sarah frowned, probably wondering why no praise for her kid was forthcoming. I was about to ask about taking you home when Sarah said in a superior voice, "I told you, your little girl would be okay. You were the one missing her."

I opened my mouth to argue but realized she was right. My world revolved around you. Parting from you, even briefly, was a tremendous strain on me.

The teacher smiled at me kindly. "Did you enjoy your break when Sophie was away?"

If I were a porcupine my quills would have stood at attention at her words. I fairly bristled. "Sophie is an absolute joy." I sniffed. "She is not a burden."

I only meant—" the teacher said, but I cut her off with an icy stare.

Sarah stared at me like I was from another planet, and the teacher's smile disappeared. "Wait here," she said and went back inside.

"Why did you have to be so rude?" Sarah snarled. "She was being kind."

Sarah was right. I felt miserable. *Foot in the mouth, again*, my brain hammered. Distracted, I stared inside, admiring the colorful interior despite my dark mood. The first thing I spotted were children sitting in a circle, clapping their hands to the tune of *Baby Shark*, imitating the youthful teacher clapping her hands in the center. I smiled as I tried to look for you.

As my gaze skimmed the room, I noticed that behind the children were light wood tables with colored borders around the edges, grouped around the centre. The chairs matched the colored edges of the tables. *Subtle but bright all the same.* I could imagine the children seated on the tiny chairs, meticulously concentrating, creating something from pebbles, or small pieces of wood, or working with paints and making a brilliant mess. There were drawings and paintings displayed around the room, bearing testimony to their artistic efforts. In addition to the vibrancy the children brought to the spacious room, their drawings and paintings on display added a splash of color, bringing a delightful cheer. Then, being a writer, I had to smile seeing stacks of colorful books in every corner. I imagined the teacher sitting in the middle of the classroom, narrating a story, replete with voices and actions. It didn't take much to imagine myself in her place.

Someone cleared their throat, and I realized that you were standing in front of me expectantly. "Mama," you said, raising your chubby arms, indicating you wanted to be carried.

Lifting you, I inhaled a whiff of baby shampoo and the rose fragrance of the bath bomb. "I missed you," I mumbled, burying my face in your neck.

"It tickles," you squeaked, and wriggled in my arms.

I felt something cold jab my neck. "Ouch, Sophie what's in your hand?" I leaned back and looked at you.

"I brought you a present, mama." Your eyes shone as you handed me a stone painted in bright hues.

I teared up. You had made me something. My daughter had not forgotten me.

"Miss, please move to the side," the teacher said stiffly.

Looking at her grim face, I realized it was too late to salvage a relationship with her. My winning personality had just pushed me to the top of her 'moms-I-dislike' list, and I could do nothing to change that. I would have to wait until kindergarten to build bridges with a new teacher or pray they changed this one. I'd been a fool, and hoped you wouldn't have to pay the price.

But then you turned, "I wanna say bye to my teacher," you said and went from my arms to the arms of the woman standing before me, whose name I later learned was Gail. The teacher's face crinkled with affection, and she laughed and joked with you. When you both started singing, '*Chubby cheeks, dimple chin* …' I realized how wrong I had been. I'd been prejudiced against Gail for no fault of hers. My only salvation was she couldn't read my mind.

It turned out that the crying little boy was Nick, Sarah's son. He brightened as soon as he saw Sophie and waved shyly. Sarah and I exchanged numbers, any animosity from our earlier interaction gone in the face of the warmth between our children. In the future, we would see a lot of playdates at the park, zoo, and our respective homes. Nick would become your best friend.

Dear Diary

I think Nick is my best friend. He is very nice to me. He is friendly to everyone. But the other children are not always nice to him. Nick is very bad at math. The teacher never shouts at him, but when he makes mistakes, the other kids laugh. I don't feel like laughing. I want to protect Nick and I wish I was a dragon; then, I would breathe fire on the other kids and make them shut up.

Nick's mom gets angry with him sometimes. Poor Nick. I tried giving him my worksheet to show his mother. But he laughed. He said it had my name on it and his mother would know it wasn't his. "She will get even more angry, Sophie. But thank you."

Nick is always so polite, even when he is hurting. When I asked him if he felt bad when the other children laughed at him, he said, "I sometimes think I'm broken, Sophie. But I'm also good at many other things. I'm not missing something. I just have other good stuff instead."

CHAPTER 5

Nina

At the beginning of second grade, you no longer felt 'little.' It was easier to shrug off the tag of being' just out of kindergarten,' as a seven-year-old. It didn't matter to Nick, but being considered one of the 'big' kids was a huge deal to you. I remember how Nick hated numbers and you loved them. When the teacher doled out worksheets with addition and subtraction problems for numbers below twenty to check the level of her student's abilities, you attacked the worksheets (yes, attacked) with glee. Nick was not so lucky. Numbers were not his friends. Purple marks decorated his worksheets. I remember Sarah's face turning red when she saw his paper, despite the use of the gentler color. Teachers had started using purple instead of red to reduce derisive comments, mockery, and anxiety. It worked on Nick, who seemed relatively equanimous, until he saw his mother's expression. It didn't seem to work on Sarah. I quickly hid your star-filled worksheet behind my back. I didn't want to make things worse for your friend. Nick did much better when the teacher repeated the activity with blocks, which slightly appeased Sarah.

I remember you seeing Nick's downcast face and hugging him.

Initially, Sarah made excuses and kept goading him to do better. The same thing had been happening since the first grade. "Nick," she said, "We just sat with some worksheets yesterday? What happened?"

Nick's face colored as all the children in his vicinity stopped and stared at him.

"Sarah, let it go," I pleaded. "Let's go home."

Her eyes burned with tears of disappointment, and Nick refused to stop staring at his feet. Both entered the car —Sarah reluctantly and Nick with relief.

At home you wouldn't touch your favorite spaghetti Bolognese. Instead, your fork pushed the food from one corner of the plate to the other. I observed you out of the corner of my eye waiting for you to tell me what was bothering you.

"Why do some of the kids call Nick 'stupid'?

I took a deep breath. "My darling, your friend is a smart boy. But there are different kinds of smarts. I believe our darling Nick has a problem with numbers. Let me look that up and then talk to his mom. How about that?"

"You would?"

"Why wouldn't I, sweetheart? Nick is your best friend and I love him, too."

"I don't looove him." You giggled. "Yuck. Nick says his mom has to remind him to have a bath every day. How can I love a boy like that?"

I almost choked on my spaghetti but kept my face serious and nodded. "You're very wise indeed. Let's forget about loving boys and leave that for when you're fifty."

"Fifty? I will be so old. Mama, you're mean." You aimed your fork and threw a large glob of spaghetti at me. *Like the old days,* I thought as I remembered the food fights of your babyhood.

"Sophie, your aim is getting better," I said as a single thread of spaghetti from your plate landed on my nose. We glowered at each other, then burst out laughing, shoving the rest of the food into our mouths.

The next day I met Sarah for coffee.

"Sarah, do you think Nick is struggling a bit at school?"

"He just needs to work a little harder. He is in tears every time he sits to do his math homework. I have to keep reminding him that boys don't cry."

"Why shouldn't he cry? Console him, of course, but let him cry."

"It's easy for you to say. You have a daughter who rarely sheds a tear." Sarah's eyes were hard.

"But her mother more than makes up for it. I can cry at the drop of a hat." I smirked.

Sarah smiled and the tense atmosphere between us eased.

"I looked up Nick's problem. As I understand from Sophie, he is fine with reading and everything else except numbers, right?"

Sarah nodded, her face a mask of concentration.

"That's good," I continued.

"What could be good about that? Why does he have a problem with numbers?"

"Most children who have a problem with numbers usually also have a problem with reading. But Nick seems to have a… learning disability linked only to numbers. I don't know for sure, but I think you ought to consult the school counselor."

"My son isn't disabled." Sarah glared at me and stood up, pushing away from the table.

"Calm down and sit, Sarah. Let me talk to you. There is a lot at stake for Nick here. I think he has something called 'dyscalculia.'"

"Is it… like dyslexia?"

"In a way. While dyslexia is related to trouble with language, dyscalculia has to do with trouble with numbers and math."

"I've never heard of it." Sarah ran her hand through her hair. "What should I do?"

"Mark and you should meet with the school counselor, and perhaps a learning specialist. They will consult Nick's teacher and together, they will find tools to make it easier for him."

She raised her eyebrows. "Tools? Like what?"

"There are ways things could be made easier for him. Simple things, like giving him extra time at sums, allowing the use of a calculator, perhaps some extra coaching, you know, stuff like that. Nick will be fine. He is an intelligent and hardworking boy. But we are jumping the gun here. First, meet the counselor. I'm just another mom. I can't do a diagnosis."

"You're more than that, much more. You're a good friend. I shouldn't have gotten angry with you."

"It's fine. Sophie and I love Nick and want the best for him."

Sarah nodded. "You're right. It wasn't Nick's fault. The poor kid tries so hard. I must make it up to him."

"You're his mother, and you love him no matter what. Who said being a mother is easy? Sometimes we, too, are learning as we go along. We might make mistakes. We are not perfect. So, don't blame yourself. Get Nick the help he needs, and he will be fine."

Dear Diary

I think I was a little mean to Nick today. He wanted to play, but my friends were coming over. Tammy is the queen of all the girls, and I want to impress her. Mom promised to give us her makeup, and I was so excited. This would please Tammy. I was almost hopping in one place. I couldn't wait for the girls to come over. Nick looked so sad when he walked away that I wanted to stop him and say sorry, but I didn't. Did I do a bad thing?

Tammy says that Nick ought to play with other boys. He shouldn't hang out with me all the time. I agreed. But to tell you the truth I secretly did not like what she said. It was okay if Nick had other friends, but I liked him hanging out with me. So, what if I am a girl?

Now I'm worried. What if Nick finds another best friend? A boy! I like playing with the girls. We have sleep overs and play dates, but Nick is also a lot of fun. I hope he stays friends with me forever.

CHAPTER 6

Nina

By the time you and Nick were eight, you, my dear, took Nick for granted. He was your shadow, always hovering.

"Nick, my friends are coming over to play. Even Tammy has agreed to come. Can we meet later?" You fluttered your eyelashes, the picture of innocence.

"I don't like Tammy. I find her yucky," said Nick.

"She is so beautiful and elegant. I wish I were more like her. You know nothing, Nick." You sounded wistful but also a little angry. "Aren't there any boys you can hang out with?" you asked, playing with your ponytail, a saccharine sweet smile plastered on your face. "I don't mind, you know. You can have other friends."

"There are boys I know. I like hanging out with you better." A blush stained his cheeks.

Oh, boy, Nick. Don't wear your heart on your sleeve like

that. It's too soon. I pleaded with him silently.

You beamed at him. "I promise to help you with your math homework later."

He smiled shyly. "Thank you, Sophie." He continued staring at you with adoration, but you were already turning away thinking of the dress-up party you had planned with your friends. I was probably the only mother willing to allow a gang of eight-year-old girls unlimited access to her makeup. My expensive cosmetics would be ruined, and there would be a giant mess to clean up, but I didn't care. Who liked makeup anyway? And wasn't the makeup-free look the fad right now? Most of all, if it made you happy, I was game.

Meanwhile, I couldn't help noticing that you were sending Nick a message in your own subtle way—'Don't be dependent on me. I can hang out, but not all the time.' *Sophie darling, be careful what you wish for.*

"And I'll bake cookies," I chipped in, looking up from my laptop. The words were flowing, and Bella and Christian were now on their fourth adventure. The readers were lapping up the *Deadly* series.

"Thank you, Nina." Nick threw me a bright smile. "I hope the writing goes well." *Ever the gallant gentleman.* "And thank you again, Sophie." He bowed slightly and slipped out of the door.

Don't be shocked by the 'Nina' bit. I insisted your friends call me by my first name. I didn't want to be Mrs Taylor to them. My first book was published under the name Nina

Taylor, and I was stuck with it, but whenever possible to whomever possible I was going to be Nina.

You and I exchanged glances and burst into a fit of giggles. "Which kid talks like that, Mom?" You shook your head, your lip pursed. "And behaves like that? Nick is sure weird sometimes."

"A good weird," I added, but you only rolled your eyes.

Nick took your advice to heart and started hanging out with the boys in the neighborhood. The transition happened so gradually that you barely noticed at first. Then came the realization that he was a natural at football. It was football season, and he took to the game like a fish to water even though the other boys in his circle had been playing since they were four or five. As a result, they gave him a warm welcome. Nick joined the school team, pursuing his love for football, and Mark, his dad, also enrolled him in a football club.

When Nick was at our house, a boy called Kyle would often turn up and ring the bell.

"Mrs. Taylor, may I speak with Nick?"

"Sure, honey but next time call me Nina. I go by Nina not Mrs. Taylor."

His eyes widened. "I get to call you Nina?"

"Why not? It's my name, isn't it?"

Nick came to the door, and I returned to your side in the kitchen where we all had been prepping a cake but try as we might to pretend everything was normal, we couldn't help overhearing Kyle's strident tones by the door.

"Dude, why are you hanging out with a girl? When we don't have practice, we could play video games at my house or yours."

You and I leaned forward, straining to hear Nick's reply but we couldn't hear his softer response.

But there was Kyle again.

"Hey, I thought I was your best friend. A girl is your best friend? You're funny Nick. But the invitation remains. Come over when you want to."

As Nick returned to the kitchen, you and I tried to appear engrossed in stirring the batter.

"What did he say?" you asked curiously.

Nick only smiled. "He wanted to hang out."

"Anything else?"

Was my little detective persistent or a glutton for punishment?

"No," he said, but his face colored.

"Kids, let's get this cake moving along otherwise you will be eating bread for tea," I said quickly, eager to save Nick from the coming inquisition.

You both let out a loud 'No,' and all was well again.

It happened slowly. Nick spending hours at a time at our home became a thing of the past, but every evening, without fail, his dad's Range Rover would stop outside our house, a weary Nick would get out, and his dad would drive off to park the car, only a couple of houses away. Nick would come to the door, and ring our doorbell, and you would rush to open it. He and you would chat for a few minutes. On the days that his family had a late dinner, he would have some milk and cookies and then trudge home. But he made sure he saw you every evening.

"Mom, do you think Nick still likes me? Am I still his best friend?" you asked.

"I believe Nick will always be your best friend."

"Sometimes I feel that Kyle from school is his best friend. You know the guy who used to ring our doorbell all the time? They even sit together at lunch."

"But you have your girls, don't you? Angela, Tammy, Helen and Karen."

"Yes, I do. But…"

My voice turned gentle. "If you don't have time to hang out with Nick, do you expect him to sit around waiting? He's had to make other friends too. Don't you want him to be happy?"

"Oh, Mom, of course I do."

"Then don't worry about it. He will always be your best friend but also have other friends. That's the way it should be. Just because he cares about or spends time with them doesn't mean he doesn't care about you."

Your nose was all scrunched up as doubt filled you. But you smiled. "Thanks, Mom."

You continued to enjoy your play dates with your girls but occasionally, I would see you peeping out of the window, trying to catch a glimpse of a boy you once had no time for. And I knew, if you got to exchange all the new friends you had made for Nick to hang out with you like he once did, you would.

Dear Diary

Mom is all I have. But she likes her books so much. When she finishes writing a book and the first few copies come, she rushes to the front door to greet the postman. And she lets me have the first copy out of the box. They sit on my shelf above my bed, and I gaze at the covers remembering the tales she told me contained within. I know this is stupid to say, even to you, but what if the characters she writes about come looking for her because they want her to stay with them forever? When she tells me stories, she talks about them as though they are real. What if she goes to live in one of her books and can't take me with her? What will I do? I will be all alone. I know I am being silly, but sometimes I feel I am competing for my mom's attention with the people from her books. She gives so much time to them. I'm not saying she is a bad mother. She is a very good one. I try hard not to disappoint her by getting good grades so she never leaves me. I want to be her perfect girl. But even though I try so hard, I still make her sad sometimes.

I saw her face when she learned Nick was a part of the drama club and I was in set design. Although she tried to hide it, I knew she was upset. She would have liked me to be in drama, too. She assured me that it was okay, but I felt terrible. I always want my mom to be happy, and I don't want to be the reason she is sad.

I feel jealous sometimes when people try to get Mom's attention. My friend Tammy says people only notice me because my mother is famous. Miss Andrews is a fan of my mom's and keeps asking if she can meet her or if Mom will sign her books. She is my teacher. Why does she want to meet my mother? I keep saying no. I don't want to share Mom with my teacher. The only person I am okay to share her with is Nick.

CHAPTER 7

Nina

"Nina, do you enjoy writing, or do you do it because you have to?" Nick asked me on one of those now rare occasions when he came over.

"I love writing. It helps me escape into a different world. And I like to think that my characters live in those worlds and that they might come looking for me one day."

How cool is that?" Nick clapped his hands.

I smiled, gave him a one-armed hug and ruffled his hair. Both our eyes were on you. You were silent. What's more, you looked like you had swallowed a penny, perhaps two. "Sophie, what's wrong?" Your shoulders were drooping and your lower lip trembled.

"Mom, why do you need to escape into a different world? Is this world not enough? Am I not enough?" you asked.

"I wasn't serious, my love. It's not as if the characters from my books will come to life."

Tears streamed down your face. "What if they do? What if they take you back with them, into the world they come from?"

Nick averted his eyes. He could never bear your tears.

"Sophie, you're ten. You know characters in books are fictional. They won't come to life. They will stay within their pages. And even if they came for me, I would refuse to go with them. My place is here with you. Come now, kids, it's time for a giant hug." Nick and Sophie rushed into my waiting arms, and I felt an ominous shiver run down my spine. I bustled trying to get things on an even keel again. "Nick, how are things in school? How are you finding math?"

You brushed your tears away. "We have decimals and fractions in grade five. Our teacher has also started word problems with multiple steps."

"Thanks for the update, Sophie, but I believe I asked Nick the question."

You swallowed, and your cheeks colored.

Nick rushed to your defense. "She is right, though."

"Is it okay to ask how you are coping?"

"Much better, since you spoke to my mom. I spend an hour in the math resource room each day with a tutor and she helps me a lot. And you know my parents have a tutor who comes in four times a week. Thank you for what you did."

"How do you find time for it all—sports, math, the rest of your studies?"

"Plus, drama, Mom. Nick has joined the drama team," you said.

"Football season ends in December. So, it's fine. I can manage," said Nick.

"That's excellent." I beamed. My eyebrows knitted. "And what about you, Sophie? Don't you find drama interesting?" I tried to tone down the hopeful note in my voice.

"At the beginning of drama class sign-ups, our teacher, Mrs. Arnold held a session on set-design. I found that very interesting, so I signed up for it."

"Oh."

"Mom, the spotlight doesn't have to be on me because I'm your daughter and you are famous. I'm not very good at drama. Were I to audition the likelihood of me being chosen as a tree would be high." It seemed you correctly interpreted the context of my 'oh.'

Nick laughed.

"Who said a tree is a bad thing," I protested. "We need trees. And I'm not famous." I added, my eyebrow raised.

"Mrs. Tay… sorry, Nina, our language teacher, Miss Andrews always asks about you. She has all your books. She even asked Sophie if you would sign her copies, but Sophie turned brick red and said you wouldn't."

"Nick, how dare you?" you jumped up, glaring at him, your hands on your hips, an angry little version of me. "Why are you telling tales?"

"Am not," he insisted.

I would have loved to sign the teacher's copies of my

books, but to keep harmony I said, "Sophie was right, Nick. I wouldn't sign those books. My agent organizes specific book-signing events; your Miss Andrews would have to attend one."

You triumphantly smiled at poor Nick, but your victory was short-lived because Nick was already engrossed in the book in front of him again.

Dear Diary

SOPHIE AGE 11

Yesterday was not a good day. I saw Nick looking at Daisy as though he was moon-struck. Nick and Daisy are the leads in the play, and because of that, they spend a lot of time together. I'm often sit at the side of the hall reading a book while they practice on the stage, and I see them laughing and joking a lot together. I barely turn the pages of my book as I keep staring at them.

Today I asked him about her. "Do you like Daisy?" I said.

"She doesn't mind talking about football, so I like hanging out with her sometimes," Nick said.

This was a surprise to me, and I guiltily asked, "Do you hate it that I hate football? That I never come to any of your games? You always come to the science fairs to see my projects."

"I'm sure it is not the same thing. When I come to the science fair, yours is the only project I see before leaving. If you came for a match, you'd have to sit for the entire game, and I know that would bore you."

I knew I should have stopped, but I persisted. "How much do you like Daisy?"

"I like her, Sophie. I haven't measured how much," Nick chuckled.

"More… more than me?"

"More than… Sophie, you're my best friend."

"That still doesn't answer my question."

"Boy, you sure are persistent. Okay. I like you more than anyone else."

I wanted to jump up with joy, but I was still suspicious. "Would you say the same thing if Daisy asked you?"

"She won't because she knows you are my best friend. I talk about you all the time."

"You do?" I put my hand to my heart. "Well, I think you shouldn't. Daisy might not like it."

"Why?" Nick asked.

My eyes glowed. "Because some girls are possessive. Daisy might not want you talking about me."

"But you have been talking about Daisy non-stop for ten minutes and seem very happy. So, I don't think that's true," Nick said.

I nodded my head sagely. "I'm different. Listen to me and don't mention me in front of Daisy."

"Yes, ma'am." Nick saluted.

"Don't ma'am me." I hit Nick with a cushion.

"I'm going to the kitchen for a snack. Do you want something?"

I shrugged but turned away so Nick wouldn't see my delighted smile. Somehow, he had said the right thing, and I was on top of the world.

CHAPTER 8

Nina

Things started to change when you and Nick went to the sixth grade. The two of you were still close, but Nick was increasingly involved with the drama club. You saw him in drama, but there was a world of difference between the actors and the set design teams. You guys rarely met at the same time.

I asked you about it. Your expression turned sour. "Nick likes Daisy, and she is the main lead." You shook your head, disenchantment flooding your eyes.

"Because he likes this Daisy doesn't mean he doesn't care about you. He is still your best friend, isn't he? Does Nick get upset when you work with boys in your class on your science project?" I couldn't believe it. Was jealousy already becoming an issue between you and Nick?

"His friends call us geeks."

"Even you?"

Sophie giggled. "Not to my face. Nick would beat them up."

I deepened my voice, sounding shocked. "He wouldn't."

"He had better," she said, her tone lined with steel.

I wanted to discourage any notions of violence. "I don't think being called a nerd or geek is bad. It means you are more interested and fluent in a topic than others. I would take it as a compliment. Nick is a member of the drama club. Couldn't he be called a nerd too?" I said hopefully.

Sophie's tone turned impatient. "He plays football, Mom, and that excuses him from the 'nerd and geek' club."

It was time to play the mom card. "I think you should start making more friends like Nick has. Talk to and hang out with more girls and boys. If you do that, Nick's friendships won't bother you, because you will be busy with your own life.

"I don't want to," you said and fled to your room leaving me wringing my hands.

Dear Diary

SOPHIE AGE 12

Today, when Mom said she wasn't sure about me playing video games, I told her why I liked them. The truth is, videogaming makes me feel like I'm fighting monsters. It's fun finding their weaknesses and then defeating them. She looked so surprised when I told her what I thought.

She doesn't mind chess even though she is terrible at it. I'm tempted to lose purposely, whenever I play with her, but she won't like it. She is the mother, and she feels superior even if she loses as long as it is fair. She is funny like that.

And oh, I forgot to mention, that Nick has a new crush —Christina. When she first came to school, Nick didn't care for her. It all started when he and I passed her in the corridor at school.

"She looks snooty," said Nick, wrinkling his nose.

"She looks like she's in high school," I said. Christina made me feel small and unpolished.

But then things began to change. Christina makes Daisy look like a saint. I miss Daisy. I wish Nick would like her again and Christina would go away. She can't stand me being friends with Nick. She hates everything about Austin except Nick. And what she hates most about Austin is me. She is okay with sharing Nick with football and his friends but not me. She is too smart to be obvious about it. That devious creature! She started dropping poisonous darts. I overheard her telling Nick, "I think Sophie feels other boys like James don't talk to her because you are always hovering around her."

What a load of rubbish!

Nick was surprised. "That's not true. Sophie can talk to whoever she likes, and anyone can talk to her."

Which was all true. I could talk to any boy I wanted. I just didn't want to, especially not to James.

But that mean girl persisted. "Probably. But don't you think you should stop hounding her every opportunity you get?"

"I don't hound her. And why should I stop hanging out with her?" Nick merely shrugged.

I was thrilled but then I caught him gazing at me wistfully.

"What?" I asked. I couldn't admit I'd overheard him and Christina.

He just shook his head.

Why couldn't I admit I'd overheard them and tell him none of what Christina said was true?

CHAPTER 9

Nina

Nick's fascination with Daisy and drama ended as suddenly as it began. For a week after that, you had this Cheshire cat smile plastered on your face.

You and Nick met whenever you could. Besides video games, the two of you started playing chess. You spent a lot of time researching chess moves like the 'Four Knights,' 'Sicilian Defense,' and 'King's Gamble,' but your favorite was the 'Queen's Gambit' because of a show by the same name. Nick did none of those things. Because of his dyscalculia, he hated reading up on chess because of all the d4s, g5s and c6's. The numbers confused him, so he played by instinct. You won many times, but Nick was no pushover. Nick had plenty of draws and victories.

When either of you played with me, I always ended up losing. Try as I did to predict my opponent's moves, I was terrible at it. I would lose essential pieces because of my defensive style playing style and be caught unawares when the queen or the bishop suddenly checkmated my king. Often, I admitted defeat as soon as I lost an important piece. When you or Nick wanted to feel good after a losing streak against each other, you played with me.

Then there were video games. You might have hated football, but you loved video gaming with Nick. It horrified me to learn that one game you played was about monsters, but you reassured me.

"Sometimes I feel afraid, Mom. What if something happened to you? You're everything to me. Would monsters come for me? This game tells me how to deal with problems and that every monster has a weakness. None is indestructible. I just have to persist until I defeat them. Then they have to go away."

"Darling, I'm never going anywhere. I will always be here for you. I will protect you from the monsters. You don't have to fight them alone." My eyes filled with tears, and I hugged you tight.

Those days were idyllic, but they passed by quickly.

Then came Christina. Your resentment toward her was clear from your diary. You disliked her from the start. You mentioned how her parents moved to Austin from New York when you were in the seventh grade. I could tell that you were sorry she came to your school.

But one day, you saw Christina and Nick in the hallway.

Christina stood leaning against the wall, and Nick stood facing her, his hand resting on the wall by her head. This upset you tremendously. Was Nick more than friends with the 'snooty girl'? What made him change his mind? You debated over this for at least two pages in your diary. It made me very sad.

Dear Diary

SOPHIE AGE 13

Today I wanted to kill myself. Things with Tammy had been going badly for some time. A while ago she demanded that I stop being friends with Nick. I protested, "But he is my best friend. My childhood friend. Christina always talks to him, but I see you laughing and chatting with her."

Tammy, always the ringleader stared me down. "You're sure?" she said playing with her ponytail. "Besides the rules don't apply to Christina. She is new and hasn't been part of our gang."

"But I have and you're trying to stop me from hanging out with my best friend," I said.

"Best friend?" Tammy bit out. "It's him or us. Choose."

"Hmmm. I could try. Would that count, Tammy? Please say yes. His mom and mine are friends. I cannot suddenly stop being friends with him completely, but I will stop hanging out. I hope it makes you happy."

Tammy and the rest of her cohorts giggled. "It's not about making me happy. I couldn't care less but it's our group's motto. If you don't adhere, you won't fit in any longer."

And then today, Tammy and my other friends put up terrible pictures of me in school. In the pictures, I barely had any clothes on. It wasn't me. I swear. It was just my face on another girl's body. Everyone believed it was me in the pictures. I could shout from the roof, and they wouldn't believe me. I was in shock. When I confronted Tammy about it, we started fighting. She hurt her head, and now I'm being blamed. I got suspended. The humiliation I faced was dreadful. I hid in the bathroom for hours, wanting to cry, but the tears wouldn't come. I knew I should have felt guilty for hitting Tammy, but didn't she push me first?

The minute I saw those pictures I stopped being a doormat and taking Tammy's crap. Why had I given this girl so much importance for so many years? I thought she would make me her best friend. But no, that's Karen. I hate Tammy. I think I wanted to hurt her even if I didn't mean to. Oh! I don't know what I am talking about. All I know is that I want to disappear and never return to school. My friends were never really my friends. They have been tormenting me for many days, and I tried to smile through it. Now they plastered horrible pictures of me all over school! I can't take it anymore. I don't know why they hate me? But now I hate myself. I don't want to exist.

Nick waited for me for hours outside the bathroom. I feel awful that I was mean to him because Tammy insisted. I don't deserve him. He is my knight in a football jersey.

"Nick, what are you doing here?" I asked him.

"Waiting for you. We missed the bus. We can either call your mom or walk home. My mother is at work."

"Would you mind walking home?" I asked. "I don't want to see my mother right now. She would be intolerable, like a wounded mother bear. I can't deal with that. Can we walk?"

"Anything you want. Come, let's go home."

"Is it okay if we don't talk? I don't want any pity or any told-you-so's," I said, my jaw set. I meant what I said.

Nick shrugged. "I don't have anything I want to talk about, so I'm good with silence."

But I changed my mind. I had to confess the truth. "I ignored you and avoided you so that …" —I took a deep breath— "Tammy would be my friend. But they are not my friends. They never were."

Nick gave me an awkward embrace and stroked my hair.

"Tammy insisted I stop talking to you. I did it to become one of them." I sobbed. "But I was never a part of their clique. I chose them over you. Oh, God, how silly I have been!"

"You are brilliant and beautiful. Tammy is stupid if she can't see you for what you are," Nick said and the two of us held hands as we walked home. "I knew you wouldn't be the one to start the fight, and I don't think you really hurt Tammy. But…" Nick hesitated.

"Tell me. Things can't get any worse," I said.

"Mrs. Thomas wants to see you tomorrow, and I think she intends to suspend you."

"Suspend me? After what Tammy did?"

"She says we have no proof."

"Then let her suspend me," I said with conviction. "I need to stay away from this place for a while anyway. I can't bear to think about those posters." Swallowing hard, I turned to face Nick. "Did you see them?"

When he wouldn't meet my eyes, I insisted. "Tell me."

"We took down every one of them."

"I guess you answered my question." The tears were falling fast.

"I know it wasn't you."

"I won't have to see them again, but everybody has already seen them. It's too late. How will I go back to school? I wish Mom would send me to another school."

"And what about me?" Nick asked.

"What about you? You have Christina," I answered, my eyes sad.

"She isn't my best friend."

"You mean that?"

"I do."

"But what about the posters?"

"That's not you, and that's all that matters. Don't worry about the others. Say you won't talk about leaving. I will be with you every step of the way." he said.

"Nick, I can't leave you, you know that. I won't go anywhere."

And that was that.

Nick thought I was okay with staying at school, but I wasn't fine at all. Forget school; I didn't want to live after what happened. But Mom needs me. She looks at me as though I will break into a million pieces. She is so scared. I have to try to be strong for her sake. Even though I have Nick, it will be so lonely in school, but I won't let my grades suffer. I won't fail my mom. She is all I have left.

I wish I had a dad. He would have fought with everyone at school and whisked me to a safe place. Mom wanted to fight for me. But I didn't allow her. What's the point? I'm a loser, and I don't want my mom to become one too.

CHAPTER 10

Nina

You never really took my advice on finding your own tribe. Perhaps it was easier for me to offer advice because I wasn't the one in your shoes. I had always been very easy to get along with. Most of the time, I was an introvert. Still at a book signing event or on social media after the initial reticence, I shed my armor and interacted freely with readers, fellow authors, and journalists. I bloomed in the spotlight, even if I was a slow bloomer.

You, my love, were not what I would call a 'people person.' I don't think I understood how tough other thirteen-year-old girls could be. I had tears in my eyes when I read how Tammy, Angela, Karen and the rest of your girl group bullied you. You got along splendidly with them for a while, but they were going through a 'boys are banned' phase and demanded you curtail your friendship with Nick. I wasn't aware of the pressure you were under until much later. Every time Nick came over, you made excuses—*I've got an assign-ment to complete. I'm tired.* Nick would shrug and leave. Soon, he stopped coming by altogether. Whenever Nick saw you, he tried to talk to you, but you could feel the girls watching you, and you were forced to give him a cold shoulder.

But Tammy was the queen of expectations; somehow you never measured up. You were always lacking from her point of view. "'Sophie, why are you wearing red? Today we decided on black,' or 'Sophie, today we were supposed to braid our hair. Why did you let yours hang loose?'"

Being a part of Tammy's gang was weighing down on you. Some days she was friendly, and on other days, that girl was as frosty as the snow queen. Tammy's unpredictable behavior left you on tenterhooks. You were a bundle of nerves. I sensed something was wrong, but didn't know what; I didn't have your diary to read then. For the first time, you had locked me out, and try as I might you wouldn't let me in. You smiled whenever you saw me watching you. You chatted with me, but your words sounded hollow. It wasn't the same. We were so close, but I could feel you pulling away. You lacked joy and were no longer the excited girl you used to be. You were not my Sophie. My precious Sophie was disap-pearing a little more each day. I asked you if you were okay, if a student at school was giving you a hard time but you only snorted in disgust.

"I'm Tammy's friend. Who would dare trouble me?"

The answer should have been obvious to me—Tammy—

but you insisted you were happy. I met your teacher, who told me you had a whole gang of friends in school. You were fine. Authorities always assume that kids being bullied are loners and have no friends but what if the ones doing the bullying were the so-called friends? What then? Who would you ask for help? Things were getting worse for you in school. The girl gang often heckled you, singled you out and called you names. You were isolated. You had no one. Your friends had turned into your bullies, making your life miserable. But you did not say a word. You dutifully went to school every day, never letting on that, things had gone so bad. I often asked why your friends no longer came over, but you made excuses. You were eating poorly, losing weight, and getting quieter each day. But you chose not to tell me anything about it. You made it your cross to bear. Should I have done more for you as your mother? Should I have stepped in instead of letting you deal with it?

One day at school things came to a head. I only pieced the story together from what I learned from Nick and the principal's office. You barely spoke to me about it. It nearly broke me. Nick told me later that someone had scribbled the message 'loser' on your locker, and there were posters all along the school corridors with a picture of you wearing the skimpiest clothes and the declaration— 'Sophie is a loser.' Now everyone would know you, but not in a good way. Your face lost color. You could keep quiet no longer. You had rushed to Tammy yelling, "Why? Why did you do this? I have been doing everything you said. Why? That's not even me in the picture. It's just my face."

Tammy stared at you coolly and then shoved you. "I don't know what you are talking about. And as for the picture, everyone thinks it's you and that's all that matters."

You fell to the ground but recovered quickly and picked yourself up. Then you ran to Tammy and shoved her. "It isn't me in those dirty pictures, and I know you put them up," you yelled at her. And that's when it happened. Tammy lost her balance and hit her head on a locker. She screamed and held her head in her hands.

You looked at her in horror as she bled all over the place. "Tammy, I'm sorry. It was an accident. I'm sorry."

"You did this on purpose because you hate me," she said. Some kids rushed to Tammy, and the rest started jeering and jostling you.

You ran to the girl's bathroom and locked yourself in a cubicle, shaking.

Nick told me that Tammy was fine, but she kept holding her head, wailing about how you pushed her.

"You shoved Sophie first," Nick accused her.

"Shut up," Tammy had screamed at him. "She hurt me. Sophie hurt me." She yelled to whoever would listen, and the surrounding crowd grew thicker.

The vice-principal, Mrs. Thomas, appeared on the scene and wanted to know what happened. And then the weeping

Tammy accused you of hurting her. Nick tried his best to intervene.

"Mrs. Thomas," Nick interrupted. "Look at these posters. They have been mocking Sophie. She did nothing wrong."

But the vice- principal's reaction was icy. She refused to believe Nick and sided with Tammy. Nick pointed at the walls. But she insisted that there was no proof that Tammy had put up the pictures. Instead, she wanted to see you in her office. Nick pleaded with her to give you time. The vice-principal seemed to have a soft spot for Nick because she smiled slightly, although it appeared more like a grimace than a smile.

"Tomorrow. But I'm sorry, Nick. I'm suspending her for a week."

"A week? But what did she do? It wasn't her fault that Tammy hit her head. And what about Tammy?"

"She is the victim. I'm not about to punish her."

Tammy grinned at Nick from behind Mrs. Thomas' back.

The posters were still up everywhere. Nick couldn't bear it any longer. They were possibly proof of the injustice against you. But seeing them again would only make you miserable, and besides, Tammy denied having anything to do with them. The school appeared more concerned about Tammy rather than you. Nick and his friends swung into action. They took down every poster, and Nick personally got a bucket of water and a cloth from the janitor and cleaned your locker. He stood by you that day, gallantly taking down the posters... I couldn't be there, but I am so grateful he was.

Otherwise, I don't know what would have happened. What you would have done?

He then stood outside the bathroom waiting for you like a gallant knight. A teacher ordered him to class, but he quietly explained to her what had happened.

"I will take this to the principal," she said.

"The vice-principal already knows. Right now, my friend is not okay, and she needs me. Mrs. Weatherly, punish me for missing class, but let me wait for her here."

She hemmed and hawed. "This is highly unusual. I will give you a note, but I will speak to the vice-principal about your friend."

"Mrs. Thomas is going to suspend her. She thinks she knows what happened. Please tell her the truth," he begged.

She hesitated. "I can't make any promises, but I will try to talk to her."

"Thank you." Nick smiled.

Mrs. Weatherly nodded and walked off. I could picture it. Nick patiently waiting outside the girls' bathroom, arms folded across his chest. As the hours passed and you didn't appear, I pictured him sinking to the floor by the wall at the side of the door, still keeping vigil.

You came out only when you were sure the entire school had left, your face red and tear-streaked.

The principal's office called me the next day, but Nick had already prepared me for what would come. I took your suspension quietly because you pleaded with me not to say anything more about the posters. It went against every emotion I felt as a mother as I knew you were hurting. I was hurting on your behalf. I don't know whether it was good or bad, but you refused to pursue the matter and defend yourself. You were convinced no one would believe you. I tried to persuade you, but you wouldn't budge. You wanted to move on. And you thought blaming Tammy would only make things worse. Everyone in school acted as though you were at fault, and not Tammy. Their hatred got to you.

"I promise you I didn't mean to hurt her," you said repeatedly.

"I know you didn't mean to hurt her. You would never hurt anyone on purpose. But are you okay?" I asked with concern.

You gave me a brave smile. "I'm fine, Mama, and this will not happen again. I won't let anyone get to me again."

Something inside you broke that day, but something also came alive. You were alone, but you were your own person. Nobody owned you. You wore what you wanted, tied your hair or left it loose. You never spoke to Tammy or her gang again. Tammy could never forgive you. She sought to ruin you that day. That you survived and even flourished a little was anathema to her. She constantly passed comments and she and her gang jeered whenever you passed by. You tried hard to erect an ivory tower around yourself. To be indifferent to those girls. But it was hard on you. They never let you forget.

Although my heart was breaking at how isolated you were, I also marveled at how strong you had become. You never said a bad word about those girls; you sat in class right in the front and gave the teacher your attention ignoring the surrounding sniggers. When Tammy and friends gossiped and giggled, you read your Kindle and put on your AirPods between classes. I know you were affected. School was for socialization, but they had ruined you socially. Yet, you never missed a day. You worked on projects with other children, many of whom had no option but to reluctantly admire you for your dedication and persistence. The other students threw pitying glances or whispered when you walked past. Except for a few, most kids were reluctant to talk to you. The popular girls had marked you, which was a good enough reason for the majority to stay away. Nick didn't care about their opinions, and was too well-liked to be ignored. But you were an easier target and were now a loner, with only Nick for company.

You held your head high and locked your tears in. Only the diary told me about your turmoil, the tears you shed, the heartache you were experiencing. You wrote at length about what Nick tried to do for you. He became your buffer. He used his popularity as a shield to try to protect you. But how much could one person do? The others would acknowledge you when Nick was around, but when his back was turned, they gossiped and spread tales about Nick and you.

"She is Nick's pity girlfriend," they commented snidely.

I wanted to scream when I read this in the diary. What the

hell is a 'pity girlfriend'? You were Nick's best friend and I damn well wanted them to remember it.

Yes, there were days when you came home, threw your bag on the floor, and burst into tears. Those days were the worst for me. I couldn't pretend that everything was fine, that my little girl was fine, and I would gather you in my arms and weep right along with you. There were no words of comfort for what you were going through and we both knew that. We would have to weather out the storm together.

If Christina ignored me earlier now, she was downright icy. She tried hard to push me away from Nick, but this battle with Tammy had only brought us closer.

Christina confronted me in the bathroom one day. "What's your problem?"

"What do you mean?" I asked.

"Why are you sticking to Nick like glue? Don't you know he is mine? Stay away. Quit hanging around him all the time. You don't want posters labeling you a 'boyfriend stealer' going up all over school, do you?"

"Nick is a person. He isn't property to talk about who he belongs to," I said.

"Merely warning you, pool-polluter," said Christina.

"What did you call me?"

"You heard me."

"Why are you calling me that name?" I asked, a line

creasing my forehead. I think I knew what was coming, and a feeling of dread bubbled inside me.

"Because Tammy told me about the time you got your period in the pool. Yuck."

My heart jumped into my mouth. "She told you? She was the only one there and swore never to tell."

"Some promises are meant to be broken," Christina cackled. "After you hurt Tammy, why should she keep your secret? Everyone knows now. And they are all having a good laugh at your expense. Does it ever stop with you? One embarrassing incident after the other. How do you show your face around here?"

CHAPTER 11

Nina

One day, you rushed home and wept in my arms, and try as I might to get out of you what had gone wrong you refused to tell me. When I wanted to visit your school, you begged me not to. When I read in your diary about your confrontation with Christina, it dazed me.

"What's wrong, darling? Please talk to me," I pleaded at the time. Why did it have to be your diary you shared everything with? Why not your mother?

But all you did was sob without saying a word. So, we stayed there silently, with me rocking you gently, cooing nonsensical words of comfort—the only thing I could do. For a long time after your conversation with Christina, you carried the feeling of being shamed all over again. You filled your diary with a harsh judgment of yourself. I wasn't sure if it was my imagination, but it felt as though you had stained the diary's pages with your tears.

As the day of the eighth-grade dance dawned, you bit your fingernails almost to the quick. Very few thirteen-year-olds had steady dates, so most students were going in groups. But you no longer belonged to one.

"Sophie, will you go to the dance with me?" Nick asked. The poor guy was walking on eggshells around you. But he figured out what you were going through and stepped up.

You were determined not to make it easy for him. "Dance. What dance?"

"The 8TH Grade Farewell Dance. We can go as friends. You don't have to have a date to go to this dance. It's not Junior Prom or anything. I... got your mom to sign the permission form, and I bought us two tickets. They were twelve dollars each."

"You got Mom to sign the permission form?" you said softly.

"I told you I did," said Nick.

"You bought us tickets?" Your voice had gone so low that Nick almost didn't hear you.

Nick's eyes grew wary. "Yes."

"And now you're asking me if I want to go to the dance? Shouldn't you have asked me before?" This time there was no disguising the sharp, angry tone.

"I'm sorry, Sophie. I didn't think. They are going to have a photo booth and lots of prizes. I thought you would love it. It's your chance to prove to Tammy that you're fine."

"I prove that every day by going to school. I prove it just by showing up. Do you think school is fun for me? Do you think I enjoy the whispers and the innuendos? I don't want to go to this stupid dance. What do you think people will say when we show up together?"

"I don't care, do I?"

"But I do," you screamed. "What about Christina?"

"What about her?"

"Won't she mind? She will make me pay if I go with you. Go to the dance with her. She is your girlfriend, isn't she? And please never ask me to a dance again."

"She isn't my girlfriend."

"She believes she is."

"Eighth grade is almost over. We are going to be in high school. You will make new friends in ninth grade. Why bother about what these kids think and say?" Nick asked you gently.

"Make friends with losers from the middle grade of other schools? The ones like me who nobody wants or cares about?" You waved your hands, almost hitting Nick. "Tormented souls of middle school find Sophie, and she will be your friend." You were practically snarling at poor Nick.

Nick shook his head, his eyes full of distress. "Don't let hate win."

You sank on the ottoman by the stairs. "I don't hate anyone but myself. I'm so tired, Nick." Tears rolled down your cheeks. "Please leave me alone."

A hurt Nick walked away. Later, you learned that despite Christina's tantrums, he skipped the dance. What hurt me the most was that your diary told me that you wanted to go. Going to a dance with Nick would have been memorable for you. But you couldn't bear the thought of Christina's hate and the derision you would face from the others. So, you hardened your heart and stamped on Nick's.

Shalini is my friend. I can't believe it; I have a friend other than Nick. She came from another school, but we hit it off right away. She makes me smile, and sometimes I even laugh. We are so different, yet we are like peas in a pod. We both are pretty sheltered, but her mother is very strict compared to mine. Another thing is that Shalini is usually even-tempered, but sometimes she sulks if she feels left out. She has a FOMO (Fear of Missing Out.)

Just because I've found Shalini doesn't mean I've forgotten about the betrayal of my erstwhile friends. It still hurts. I'm fixated on Tammy, it's almost like I am the prey, and she is the hunter. I look out for her all the time—where she goes, what she does, and who she hangs out with. I hear her laughing when she finds something funny, and I know she has just made fun of somebody.

Tammy hasn't forgotten about me either. She keeps up

her mean jabs every time I pass her. Her minions try to trip me at lunch. Every day I wonder what new nightmare might await me. While nothing bad has happened again, I can't help feeling this dread in the pit of my stomach.

I HATE HER.

Nina

Christina was still a part of Nick's life in freshman year. Her presence didn't bother you, at least not in a way that was visible to me. You didn't seem to care anymore. There was nothing I could say to you. You seemed to be doing everything right. You were well on your way to becoming an honors student and would have no problem with advanced placement in the higher grades. But a vital part of you was missing. Where was that spark, that joie de vivre in my girl? The light that used to shine in your eyes had disappeared. Nick would come around, trying hard to make you laugh, and you would reward him with tiny smiles. That boy yearned for those smiles of yours, as did I. I kept asking you if there was anything I could do for you, anything you needed, but you would smile at me sweetly and say you were okay. What was I supposed to do? It was as if I couldn't reach my little girl anymore. You had locked yourself away so firmly that nothing Nick or I did reached you.

During those times, I was thankful for Shalini. If I expected that in freshman year, you would somehow miraculously acquire a whole gang of friends, I was wrong. After what happened in middle school, a part of you had withdrawn into a shell. You found one girl you liked—Shalini. She remained your steady friend from when you were freshmen until you were juniors. She was a quiet girl, quite the antithesis of Nick. Nick mostly shunned his books, but Shalini loved them, and she was in almost all the same classes as you—French II, Algebra I, English I, and Biology. Shalini was shy, and the only one who called me Mrs. Taylor. With her brown eyes and waist-length dark hair, which she loved to plait, I adored her. When I insisted, she call me Nina, she politely declined.

"My mother would have a fit if she heard me calling you by your first name, Mrs. Taylor. If we were in India, I would have to address you as auntie." She laughed when I looked aghast. "Don't worry, I won't call you that."

I glanced at you and almost fell off my chair to see you chuckling. This girl was magical. Her presence was so unassuming and non-threatening that you were almost your old self. Nick and I were part of your past. You hesitated to let go in front of us because you believed that we had witnessed your public humiliation. But Shalini knew nothing about the incident; if she had heard about it through the grapevine, she said nothing. Tears threatened to spill. How could my daughter not trust me? Did you think I judged you for what happened? My eyes widened. Instantly, I realized it was probably my fault, bringing up things you did not want to think about. And Nick behaved like you were fragile not the friend he used to push around and joke with at the drop of a hat. Both of us were so careful about what we said around you. Trying hard to treat you tenderly, we had done the one thing you dreaded—being treated differently. I was thankful for Shalini's presence. If not for her, you would have had no one else. I was your mother, but seemed to be persona non grata in your books.

Dear Diary

SOPHIE AGE 16

My mother is driving me mad! She watches me all the time. I think she is afraid of what I might do. It's my fault, as I've often woken her up in the middle of the night with my screams. I have nightmares about Tammy. The things that happen to me in my dreams get progressively worse. At that moment, they feel so real. Hence the screams. Sometimes Tammy comes at me with a knife, and at other times, she throws me off a cliff. Then there are times when Tammy isn't there, but I am standing amid a circle of kids, and they all are laughing and jeering at me.

Mom is afraid for me and she is not wrong. I'm not entirely okay. There are times I lapse into the nightmares even when I am wide awake. It's been over two years since the incident in school, but Tammy and her friends never let me forget. Even if they disappeared off the face of the Earth, I doubt I would forget. Instead of things getting better, they have only turned worse. I'm drowning in my misery, and I don't know what I can do about it. I frequently think I needlessly take my frustration out on Mom. Who else do I have? What else can I do? I find my mom crying in a corner of the house where she thinks I might not see her, and I hate what I'm doing to her, but I can't help it. Although I need to talk about what happened, I can't bring it up. I can't let go. I am stuck in the past, and I believe my future grows dimmer each day.

CHAPTER 13

Nina

You made it through sophomore year. I made it through sophomore year but barely. Obsessing about the changes in my baby girl left me with very little energy for writing the *Deadly Series*.

You should have been able to put the incident behind you by now. Why hadn't you? Little did I know that others around you never let you forget. Every day, what happened a couple of years ago haunted you. You'd learned to hide your feelings, but as your mother I knew my baby was hurting.

"Why aren't you writing anymore?" you kept asking me. That's all the few people in my life asked. The questions gave the impression that I wasn't much without my writing. Was it all that was there to my body and soul—my identity as a writer?

"It's just a small break," I lied, because the pressure of pretending everything was okay and things were hunky-dory had become too much. I was obsessed with you and making things right for you again. But how? I was your mother, yet I couldn't reach you despite how hard I tried. What went on at school was totally outside the sphere of my control. Heck, I couldn't even make things right at home. After the incident with the bullies, you went through some sleepless nights and would wake up screaming with nightmares. I stayed awake at intervals at night, listening for your screams. I didn't want to sleep peacefully and risk not being there for you.

"You're lying. I can see it in your eyes," you said, yanking me back to the present. "It's because of me. Isn't it? I'm the reason you won't write anymore. How many times do I have to tell you I'm fine?"

I stared at you in dismay. "I'm sorry I made you feel that way. But I am your mother and have a right to be worry about you. Isn't it my job to be concerned?"

You snatched at my words like a dog would a bone. "See, that's what I'm trying to tell you. You watch me constantly as though I'm some tragic heroine about to have a breakdown." Your voice rose a pitch higher. "Yes, something bad happened to me. But it happens to other children too. It's not the end of the world. I know I'm different. I'm not the girl I used to be, but why can't you accept me the way I am now? Why do you keep looking for that long-lost girl? I've changed. For better or for worse, I don't know, but this is me. I know, I'm your only daughter but stop moping around the house because of me."

You were shaking so badly that I wanted to rush and embrace you in the safety of my arms.

But your last words were too much for me. "It feels like someone died, and I feel like that person is me. You make me feel that way."

My hands folded over my heart, and I recoiled. "I love you, Sophie, and I never meant to make you feel smothered. I'm so sorry." Bending my head, I stared at my shoes, waiting for you to say something, anything. But your words never came. Instead, you left the room, and I heard the door bang behind you, the ultimate confirmation that things between us were so bad that you didn't even want to comfort me or accept my apology.

At times like this I almost wished that Tim was still a part of my life. Then Sophie would have strong arms and a gentle embrace to go to when she was angry with me. But it would never be. After our divorce Tim had remarried and moved away. I think he even had kids. So, he wanted the 'wife and kids' bit. He just didn't want us. I felt so alone. Desperate, I rushed to the phone and dialed my agent, Beth. "I need to see you. I need a friend."

All she said was, "I'm coming over."

She kept her word. She was by my side within thirty minutes. Beth admonished me after I told her what happened. "We have more than enough books published, so taking a break from writing is not an issue. But Sophie is right. You are lost without your writing, and she can see that. You are making her feel like you are giving up an essential part of yourself because of her. Whatever you're obsessing over, is not good for you. You should write. You are a writer and writers must write. It's in your blood."

Being a mother is what's in my blood. I wanted to shout at her. But I remained silent and sipped my coffee. "I will write. I promise you. It might be outside the series as I'm not in the mood for Christian and Bella right now, but I will write."

She nodded sagely, sighing in relief. I knew what she was thinking. *Start writing, and then I will slowly divert you back to our money-making series.* I looked at her defiantly. I would write when I was good and ready. We'd made enough money to be okay for the future. Moreover, Beth was in talks negotiating the movie rights to my series. I would have been over the moon any other time, but you were all I could think about now.

By the time Beth left, I was almost feverish with impatience. I rushed to the study and pulled out a fresh notebook. This felt like a pen-and-paper story, not something I wanted to type. You needed a new character in your life to distract you. I couldn't find that person in real life, nor could I be that person, but I could create the individual through my writing. This would be cathartic for me even if I couldn't tell you about it. I needed to feel useful. Through my writing, I would create someone to heal your hurt. I would imagine a character who had your back, someone who was always there for you. I would fashion with words a friend who would intrigue you. Not one like Nick, who you took for granted. I was a writer, so I would write.

I should have thought about the fact that you already had that person in your life—Nick. So, what if he wasn't the least mysterious? I knew that in my heart he loved you. Why couldn't I see that detail? You just needed to lean on him more. Nick was ready and waiting. He was always there for you. He was waiting for a sign from you. Weren't you the reason he refused to commit to that Christina?

Why did I have to pick up my pen? Why did I need to interfere in your life?

Dear Diary

SOPHIE AGE 16

I just woke up from another nightmare. They are getting worse. I tried to sleep again, but couldn't let go for fear of falling back into the same dream again. So, I wrote a bit in my diary. But then I heard sounds from downstairs. I crept down afraid my mother might have been crying again. But she was in her study. I think she has started writing again.

CHAPTER 14

Nina

I turned the pages of the final diary to find it empty. Refusing to believe this was the end, I kept turning the pages, hoping to find some hidden clue as to what was going on in your mind and what really happened in those last couple of months. I needed to make sense of the conversation we had on that last day… the day I finally lost you for good. Oh Sophie, why did you stop writing? It seems I was also responsible for breaking your bond with your diary. These empty pages are my fault… they would have held the key. What happened Sophie? Will I ever truly know?

Part Two

SOPHIE

The Wall

IRA RANA

There's a wall around my heart,
Bricked one by one.
Each hurt, each pain,
has left another layer thick.
I long to tear it down,
But it is fear that keeps me still,

In the background, safe I am,
But stuck by my own free will.
And I wonder if I'll ever find
That strength, to break it wide,
To let one see the real me,
Not forced to run and hide.

CHAPTER 15
Sophie

I have reflected on these last few months in my head so many times. It can never be written down, or completely told… except to *him*. I can trust him. Him… I remember the day I first saw him. Shalini wasn't around that day, and I was trying hard to fade into the background. This was the new norm for me. It didn't matter that I was now a junior. Irrespective of the passage of time, the need to disappear was ever-present, becoming ingrained. The incident with Tammy was so long ago, but it was always in my thoughts. Every day that I came to school. I expected the worst. Nothing happened, yet a feeling of dread perpetually occupied me. From time to time, when I closed my eyes, that dismal day of my confrontation with Tammy drew me back as if I were a spectator floating outside my body. I saw my reaction to the pictures; I saw myself losing it, and finally, I saw myself rushing to the bathroom. It all happened so quickly—my life destroyed in mere minutes, and here I was years later, a shadow of my former self. If I could go back, what would I change? I'd kept running various iterations through my head, but it ended the same way each time—with me in tears.

My eyes met those of a guy in the crowd, someone I had never seen before. It was as if all the chatter and the kids around me no longer existed. He stood in the crowd, unaffected by the bustle, staring at me as though he had been willing me to look at him. His gaze was intense, and familiar. The expression on his face was sympathetic, as though he knew what I was thinking. It felt as though he knew me and felt like... wait! Did I know him? Why did it feel that way? Then someone bumped into me, and I turned away for a second. When I looked back, he was gone. I stood rooted to the ground, shocked by what had just happened, looking all around, desperate to find him.

Instead, I saw Nick and Christina, and the instinct to disappear resurfaced, but this time I didn't act hastily enough. They saw me at the same time. The comical variance in their expressions almost made me laugh. Nick's face brightened, while Christina's expression turned stormy. He rushed toward me, dragging her behind him, and enveloped me with a one-armed hug.

"How have you been? It's been days since I saw you." Obviously, this statement came from Nick, not Christina.

Nick's tone jerked me out of the stupor I seemed to have

fallen into. *He sounds so happy to see me. What did I do to deserve a friend like him?*

I stood staring at the couple until Christina cleared her throat loudly.

"Sophie, did you hear me?" Nick sounded a bit hurt. His brown eyes had a puppy dog look in them.

I hurriedly replied, giving him an apologetic look, "You saw me yesterday." *Come on Sophie, you could do better. Nick deserves a better response from you.*

"Well, it feels like a hundred years."

Nick looks even more hurt. I can't make things right. It would be best just to run away before things get worse. "I've got to go Nick. I'll catch you later," I said, rushing past the couple.

I heard Nick say, "You could have said hi. She's, my bestie."

"Ya, whatever. What did you mean by— *it feels like a hundred years*? Wear your heart on your sleeve much?" Christina said.

Even as I walked away, my back to Christina and Nick, I tried to imagine how she looked at that moment. Her eyes narrowed, her cheeks red, and her mouth downturned into a sneer. I laughed guiltily, imagining her as a cartoony figure trying to rile Nick into hating me. *As though she ever could!*

That was the day I stopped writing in my diary. *That* new boy, the one I saw in the crowd was all I could think about.

But I didn't want to write about him or talk about him. He was my secret. That night, when I went to bed, I was restless. A pair of smoky black eyes, and curly, close-cropped brown hair and bronze skin haunted my dreams. I tried to drive him away and replace him with anyone else in my mind's eye, even Nick's solid, dependable image. But I kept seeing *him* and not just seeing him. He was all over the place, his hands in my hair, his lips on my skin. I woke up with a start, and after running my hands through my hair and assuring myself that they were my hands, I lay down, but the tossing and turning started again, until finally I must have fallen into a dreamless sleep.

In the morning, Mom made pancakes for breakfast. I knew she would notice if I barely touched them, so I tried to scarf down as many as possible. Real life is not like the movies where the mom prepares a massive spread for break-fast, and all the kid eats is a piece of toast before rushing out of the door. It would never work in our house. So, eat I did.

"Sophie, you are fine, aren't you?" she called after me. "I'm glad to see you enjoyed breakfast today."

I saw the look on Mom's face and sighed. She was not done. There was something else she wanted to say. "What is it?" I dragged out.

"Nothing." She laughed, rolling her eyes.

"Okay then, bye," I said.

"Why do you have such dark circles under your eyes?" she blurted out.

"Questions. Questions. Mom, will you stop it?" Mom was

constantly worrying about my dark circles, my food, and my friends. The only thing she didn't worry about was my studies. She was a funny mother. "Don't worry, it was just a bad dream."

"How are things in school? You will tell me if someone troubles you, won't you?"

I thought of those eyes that haunted my dreams, but I knew that's not what she meant.

"Mom, I'm not a kid any longer. I know how to handle Tammy. I ignore her. She gossips about me, yes. She tries to spread tales. But she doesn't want to draw too much attention to herself. I can deal with it. Don't worry."

There was no point in rushing to school, I thought as I once more scanned the empty corridors. At least, it was empty to me, though it was milling with kids because the one person I was looking for was nowhere to be seen. *Which grade was the mysterious boy in? Which class was he in? Why couldn't I spot him?*

"Hi!"

It was Nick. Not the person I was looking for. For once the comfort I usually felt when I saw him was missing. I felt nothing. He could have been a stranger walking up to me.

"Do you want to hang out this evening?" he asked.

I was free but my mind was preoccupied. I wouldn't be great company. "Not really. I have plans with Shalini."

"Oh. I guess I will see you later then."

Shalini thumped my back. "Do we have plans today that I don't know about? Have I forgotten something?"

Before I could stop myself, I gently slammed my head against my locker. I had completely forgotten to tell Shalini I'd lied to Nick. "What did you say to him?" I asked my eyes round.

"You know I've got your back. I told him we had plans, and I forgot."

"Do you think Nick knew I was lying to him?"

She shook her head. "I admit I saw something in his expression. But no, he didn't suspect you lied. He was probably hurt you didn't think to include him. Shalini looked perplexed. "Why would you lie? You could have just said no. Nick's a big boy."

I couldn't hide my crestfallen expression. "I've been saying no too often lately."

"Why?"

I stared at my feet glumly. "Christina hates us hanging out together."

"Who cares what she likes? They are not an item. At least that's what I think. Christina wants it badly but Nick he has eyes only for—" Shalini cut herself off mid-sentence.

When I raised my eyebrows, she just shook her head. "But they are together so often," I said.

"Have you asked Nick if Christina is his girlfriend?"

"If she isn't, then does it mean he is just stringing her along?" I almost shouted. "Because I know Christina believes she is Nick's girlfriend. She is so possessive of him."

Shalini sighed and put an arm around my shoulder. "I get it. You don't want to get into a brawl with yet another girl."

I started and stared at Shalini with my mouth hanging open. "Does that mean you know about Tammy?"

Her consternation was palpable. "I hope I haven't upset you. I know, and I feel for you but let me tell you I don't feel sorry for you. You gave as good as you got."

I bit my lip as I dwelt on what she said. Finally, I whispered, "You don't think it was my fault?"

"It's Tammy's fault not yours. That girl really has it in for you. Let's stay away from her. And don't worry, like I said, I've got your back. Why don't we hang out at Zilker Park if you have nothing to do? We don't have to go swimming. We could walk in the Botanical Garden or by the water's edge. What do you say?"

I usually loved hanging out at Zilker Park, but I hesitated. "How about I let you know later?"

I could always count on Shalini to be non-judgmental and undemanding. "That works." She left for class, but not before giving me a tight hug.

CHAPTER 16

Sophie

It was a long way home, but I decided to walk back. I could easily catch a ride with Nick but there was Christina to contend with, and in the little time I saw her, I could barely tolerate her. I hated myself for hating her, but I did. She was another person to add to my list of those I despised.

Even though I had my driver's license, Mom was dithering about getting me a car. I think it was because she had lost her brother in a tragic car accident when she was just a kid. Her past was something I felt she locked deep inside. She only talked about it once because I'd pestered her about my lack of cousins. That's when she reluctantly told me about her brother. I knew nothing of my dad's family. I'd never even met my dad, and although sometimes I felt pangs over his absence, I knew it hurt my mother too much to talk about him. So, I sealed my lips and never asked. But who was I to judge? Could I speak about what happened to me in middle school? I'd buried it deep in a corner of my heart, and I wouldn't let go of the pain. I said I was over the incident, but I wasn't. Mom said she was over the trauma of her brother's death, but here I was with no car. Does one really get over a tragic event?

I felt selfish for dwelling on my need for a car when Mom had something so big to cope with every day of her life. She must miss her brother so much though she never spoke about him, and there were no photographs in the house. If me walking home or taking the bus made my mother feel better, then so be it. One day, I would have to drive, Mom couldn't avoid it. But perhaps that day wasn't today. Right now, I'd gladly kick that can down the road for my mother's sake.

My thoughts meandered as I walked home, taking in the scenery. It was early September, and we had been back at school from our summer break since mid-August. School started early for me. Junior year was off to a slow but good start. It could still be called summer because the grass in front of the one and two-story homes was dry. All the homes were beautiful made of red brick or white limestone. I preferred the red brick ones. Cars whizzed by as I walked down a winding, sloping, hillside road, and I had to watch where I was going. It wouldn't do to get too lost in my thoughts.

I giggled as I caught sight of a deer staring at me from behind a tree, and my laughter startled me because I so rarely laughed. I instinctively waved at the deer, and it, appearing unfazed, ignored me and slowly returned to the undergrowth behind. A bench was coming up ahead, and I debated whether to sit down and rest my weary legs since I still had a distance to go. I sighed deeply when I saw that it was occupied. It wouldn't do to sit near a stranger. They might start a friendly conversation, which didn't mean anything, but I wasn't in the mood. Besides, I didn't like strangers in my personal space. Then I saw it was a boy. He looked up and his eyes met mine.

It was *him*—the boy from school. I'd been trying to spot him all day, and here he was, wiling away his time on a bench of all places. What if I had taken the bus? I'd have missed him altogether. I forgot that I didn't know him, that he didn't owe me any explanations. All I could think about was how irritated I was that he had disappeared.

"What are you doing here?" I snapped, entirely forgetting I had no right to question him.

He gave me a bemused smile. "Sitting on a bench."

"I can see that." My tone was still shrewish. "I meant, what is your reason for being here? Why are you here?" I waved my hands around, pointing at nothing in particular. He understood what I meant. He wasn't stupid.

"Do you want me to admit I was waiting for you?" His eyes twinkled. "Okay, I was waiting for you."

My face grew hot, my arms snuck behind my back, and my fingers curled inward. I wanted to disappear. Was my thinking so transparent? "Why would I want that?" I blustered. I would not admit that I'd been looking for him all day.

"So, you aren't happy to see me?" His tone had a finality to it that I didn't like. Was he going to stand up and walk away? I was sure I didn't want that even if I wouldn't admit to being happy to see him.

I shook my head in exasperation, not being the type of girl to play coy. But his directness confounded me, and I wasn't sure what to say. "I was going to take the bus." It slipped out before I could stop myself.

"I'm glad you didn't." He grinned.

I stared at him, almost inhaling the sight of his tall, lithe frame. Cute boys were in abundance at my school. I enjoyed looking at them, but none made me feel like this guy did, and I wanted to hold on to the feeling. *What about Nick?* I didn't like thinking about Nick in front of this hunk of a guy, but I would be the first person to admit that Nick was my impossibility. He would always be just a little out of reach. And there was our friendship to think of. What would happen if I told Nick I liked him, and he didn't feel the same way? Our friendship would never recover.

"Are you going to say something or just stare at me?"

His voice drew me back to the present. "I was thinking. But the fact remains that I don't know you, do I?"

"Is that important?" He gave me another crooked grin. "Tell me, did you look for me at all today?"

I grimaced at the knowing look on his face. "We've barely spoken for a minute, and everything is about you."

His eyes twinkled again. "Because unlike most girls, you don't seem to be the type who wants things to be about you.

Rather, you hate the attention and would probably bolt. You wouldn't still be here talking to me."

He was right. I hated being in the spotlight. "What makes you say that?"

"Just a guess."

"Well, it doesn't mean I like talking about you. *Did I look for you? Did I miss you?*" I mimicked his tone. "These are not questions I want to answer," I pressed my lips together.

"Perhaps because I would like the answers too much if you were truthful." He gave me a sly look and laughed. He then held his hand over his heart and gave me a puppy dog look.

I shook my head at his self-assurance, but he made such an endearing picture that I couldn't help but smile. "Don't people need to know each other to stand around talking like this?"

"That's a bit of a conundrum." He scratched his head, his eyes never leaving mine. "Without talking how would you get to know me?"

Something he said struck me as odd. "I need to get to know *you*?" I stared at him, dumbfounded. Why is this one-sided again? "Don't you want to know me, too?"

"I know you. Or at least I know enough." He grinned.

His confident reply made my smile waver. *He knew me.* Then it hit me. He knew me. *What did he mean? Was he was toying with me? Was he one of the kids who had witnessed my humiliation at Tammy's hands? Did he still remember? Had he seen me fall to pieces? Had he seen my pictures on the school walls? Or worse was he one of Tammy's cohorts teasing me on her behalf?* A faint feeling engulfed me and I felt clammy. *I know you. I know you.* His words reverberated in my head. That's why he was staring at me at school. Even if he wasn't Tammy's friend perhaps, he recognized me from videos of my infamous pictures that circulated online. Mom tried her best to get them scrapped, but remnants always remained, and I would often find boys randomly staring at me and whispering among themselves. Shalini, knowing about my past hadn't bothered me much, but this boy… it mattered. I had been so wrong about him. He was one of them. One of my tormentors. I straightened my shoulders and arranged my expression into a neutral mask. "I've got to go," I whispered and rushed past him before he could say another word.

CHAPTER 17
Sophie

Shalini and I ended up going to Zilker Park. We invited Nick too, my earlier reservations forgotten. I decided to have a good time, even if Christina tagged along but she didn't. It was only the three of us. I think she didn't want to spend an extended amount of time with me. It was no skin off my nose. Nick drove us there. I shrugged off the invisible coat of melancholy that usually enveloped me and was determined to be a cheerier version of myself. But my efforts to revitalize that 'chirpy version' must have rung false because, on the drive there, Shalini and Nick kept giving me surprised glances every time I laughed.

Much later Nick and I were sitting on the great lawns. Shalini had brought along a hammock, and she was several feet away having a nap with her headphones on.

"What's the matter?" I whispered, my voice cracking. "Never seen anyone laugh before?"

Nick shrugged. "None of my jokes were that funny. Are you upset? Did someone say something to you? Were you covering it up by laughing?"

Why did he always believe I was someone's target? I turned my head away. *But he was right. I was upset.* "I'm fine, Nick. Stop playing bodyguard. Don't you tire of it? I'm not 100% okay, but I want to pretend I am. Is that so wrong? I'm tired of being the victim. I'm not doing this for you or Shalini but for myself. So please, no more analyzing. Just play along."

Nick said nothing for a long time, but then he smiled. "If that's what you want, that's what we will do. Laugh away. In fact, I will go right ahead and join you when I feel like laughing. What's the point of being sad? When Shalini wakes up let us go kayaking. We will make fools of ourselves when the kayak tips over and we get drenched. It will give us something to laugh about."

Nick listened to me. This was nothing new, and I wanted to hug him, but Christina's recently issued dire warnings echoed in my head and I satisfied myself by grabbing his hands with both of my own and smiling at him warmly.

We had a splendid time. Kayaking on Lady Bird Lake was a lot of fun. I loved the tranquil waters of the lake and the stunning views it offered. People were jumping into the water at random spots, making a big splash. But rather than checking out the swimmers, spotting turtles sunning themselves on fallen logs by the water's edge was the most fun for me. Several people were around in canoes and kayaks and a large group enjoyed stand-up paddling. I wasn't confident enough to try that. Overall, it was pretty crowded but still scenic. We tried to stick together but I was immersed in the sights and sounds and soon lost sight of Nick and Shalini. I was in an isolated bubble despite all the people around me. I tried to head for the spot where Barton Creek flowed into the lake as it offered a magnificent view of the limestone cliffs and was by far my favorite spot.

The only uneasy moment was when I spotted Nick far ahead chatting with a paddler wearing a neon T-shirt and black shorts, whose back was to me. He had curly brown hair and cut a very familiar figure. Could it be *him*? I stared at them willing him to turn. But he never did. They chatted and then he pulled away and headed to the shore.

"Nick! Nick! Wait up," I shouted and started rowing in a frenzy to catch up with him.

"Where's the fire, Sophie?" Nick asked when I caught up.

"Who… were you talking to?"

"Just some random guy. I didn't even catch his name."

It was time to get to the crux of the matter. "What did he tell you? Did he ask about me?"

"About you? Not at all. Why would he? What's the matter Sophie? Why are you all hot and bothered about this guy?"

"Nothing." My shoulders slumped. I looked sharply toward the shore. "I thought he was Tammy's friend."

"Tammy's friend?" Nick furrowed his brow.

"Forget it. I was being silly."

"Guys. Guys. Wait for me." It was Shalini. The guy paddling was no longer in sight, and Nick looked like he would love to change the topic. "Let's go back to the shore together, shall we? Shalini called out. "What is the point of coming together and separating on the lake? From her tone, I could feel a reprimand coming. "And from the looks of things the two of you were together, and I was alone."

"No," I protested. "I just found Nick."

"Oh, okay then." She seemed a bit mollified. "Let's head back."

I could feel Nick's eyes on me. He must think I'd lost it, going on about Tammy like that.

"The kayaks didn't tip over," I whispered, and he burst out laughing, the strangeness between us forgotten.

Sophie

The next day at school I didn't mind admitting that the outing at Zilker Park had done me a good. Perhaps pretending to be happy was a step in the right direction toward actually feeling happy. I felt a little lighter as I walked down the corridor, and I was almost dancing to a tune in my head. Distracted, I rammed into someone coming from the other direction. Before I could step away, I felt a pair of powerful arms hold me and move me slightly backward away from their body. And then I was looking up into *his* eyes, a polite apology dying a quick death on my lips. I stared up at him my mouth hanging open. He wore a quizzical expression as he stared back at me, his hands still holding my arms just above the elbows. I felt his thumbs gently grazing the rough skin of the joints between my hands and arms—or was that my imagination? I should take a quick peek to be sure, but I couldn't seem to look away.

"Are you still mad at me?" he murmured, his eyes tender. His voice was so low I was not sure if he had spoken. All the bluster and boldness of our first meeting seemed to have fizzled out. Today he was just a boy standing before me— what was he saying? Did he ask if I was still upset?

I thought I was done with him, but seeing him here in familiar surroundings was so unnerving that I seemed to have lost the ability to speak. Unable to say a word, I stared up at him, drinking in the sight. I could feel my hand itching to lightly caress his cheekbones, which gave his face a slightly austere appearance. He looked like I did most days—like he was getting very little sleep. I wanted to slap myself for desiring him. He was Tammy's friend. He was here to take advantage and help me make a fool of myself again.

But his eyes held genuine sorrow as he said, "I don't like how we left things last time. I've gone over it a thousand times, but I couldn't fathom what exactly I said that upset you."

There were so many things I wanted to say—*why would you toy with me like this?* Or *I missed you* or *why do I dread seeing you yet can't help wanting to see you?*

When I still didn't speak, he sighed. "Would you meet me at our bench after school?"

I didn't reply, but I think I took a deep breath. My lower lip jutted out in response, and I would have crossed my arms if he wasn't still holding them.

"Okay," he said. "I get it. You're still upset about something, but I will wait for you there every day until you decide to show up."

I pouted. "And what if I never do?"

"It will be my loss, won't it? But I don't think you'd be so heartless. You will show up." And with those words, he abruptly let go of me and walked away. I was unaware that I'd been leaning into him. Losing his support, I almost lost my balance, but just managed to steady myself by putting a hand on the locker beside me.

I was so distracted during class that once, the teacher had to call my name several times to get my attention. Shalini gave me a sharp jab (ouch, it hurt!) finally drawing my attention. All I could think of was, *what was I going to do? Would I take the bus or walk home and see if he was there waiting for me? And then what? Would I confront him about his involvement with Tammy? If I took the bus, I wouldn't be able to see if he was there as the bus took a different route from the one I walked down.*

We had a block system for classes with only three academic courses and one extracurricular in a day and school ended early. Shalini was in many of my classes, except for the extracurricular, and she kept up an endless chatter when the teacher wasn't looking, not needing me to contribute much to the conversation.

I trudged the bus steps with a heavy heart when the day

ended. I so badly wanted to see him, but at the same time, I knew avoiding the bench was the right thing to do. Moreover, I intuitively understood I wouldn't see him at school for a while, until I met him as he requested.

Sophie

Over the next few weeks, I threw myself into my SAT preparation. I had my books and a host of online resources to fall back on. I'd started preparing in my sophomore year but ever since I saw *him (why didn't I know his name?)* I'd been distracted and all my studying had fallen by the wayside. Planning to take the test for the first time in December, I had a few months to ensure I was ready. I had done pretty well in my PSATs, but this was not the time to be overconfident. If I were unhappy with my score, I'd retake it in March. Everyone else was preparing for homecoming. But I didn't like football and dances were not my thing, so I didn't think I was going.

School, bus, home and studies—this was my routine. Occasionally, I broke it by hanging out with Shalini or Nick at the mall or downtown. Once, we even made it to Barton Springs Pool at Zilker Park. I was doing everything I could to forget about *him*— perhaps waiting for me at the bench and leaving disappointed each day. Assuming he was really waiting. How, could I know? Who was to say he remained true to his word? Any logical person would give up after two or three days, if not less than that. And if he stopped coming to the bench and I didn't see him at school anymore, did this mean I would never see him again? I should have been happy. After all, this was what I wanted. Wasn't it? But no, I admitted to myself. I wanted to see him again more than anything. I couldn't help wondering, what if I didn't give him a chance and he was the one, the special someone missing from my life?

Finally, I weakened and allowed my longing to win. I was going to walk home. Most likely, the bench would be empty. After all, three weeks had passed since he promised to wait for me. But I had to do this for myself. I had to go there. I had to see he wasn't there and then I would try to move on. As I walked down the hill this time, I barely noticed anything of the passing scenery other than an armadillo that ran across the road right in front of me. Boy, was I glad when it escaped becoming roadkill. As the path meandered closer to the houses, I gradually noticed the beautiful oak trees. The leaves were usually a deep green during the summer, but since fall started, they were changing color and the mix of red, orange, yellow, and purple was such an amazing sight that, despite myself, I couldn't help admiring their deep beauty. Alas, many of these striking leaves would eventually fall off, leaving most of the branches bare for the winter. Why did all things wondrous and beautiful have to end? Why couldn't they go on forever?

And then I was there. And the bench was empty. I stood rooted to the ground as I stared. Though I'd kept telling myself it would be empty, in my heart of hearts, I'd hoped he would be waiting for me. But he wasn't and I could do nothing about it. I wanted to stamp my foot and scream, but most of all I wanted to cry. I could feel tears pricking at the corner of my eyes. But I did none of those things. Instead, I took a deep breath and prepared to walk away, but then I looked up and my face grew hot—for he stood leaning against a tree with one foot propped up against it, arms crossed, staring right at me. Oh… the embarrassment. He must have seen all the emotions flickering across my face. I could no longer pretend indifference and said a silent prayer of thanks that I'd refrained from all the histrionics I'd been tempted to indulge in moments ago.

I wanted to walk toward him, but my feet felt glued to the foot-path, and I couldn't move. Realizing my predicament, he straightened, and approached me, moving with the grace of a cat. When he was a few paces away, he stopped and seemed to devour the sight of my face. His hands were by his side, but I swear I felt like he was holding my face.

"You came," he said, his voice barely above a whisper.

"I did," I whispered back, sounding breathless and I was. "You waited." I had been so convinced that he wouldn't be here, and to find him was such a bounty that my happiness knew no bounds. I didn't know what to say or do.

"I did." He moved closer and touched me, brushing two fingers against my cheek. It was almost like the touch of a butterfly's wings, and then his hand returned to his side.

"Why won't you tell me your name?" I whined, not meaning to, but I couldn't help myself.

He laughed. It was a brilliant laugh, boisterous and unrestrained. It was the most wholesome thing I'd heard in a long time. I started laughing, too, but to my ears, it sounded brittle as though I was on the verge of tears.

"You never asked," he chided. "But now that you have, it's Tristan Corella."

"Oh." I'd always thought of him as *him*—just that. I never tried to name him, but it was worth waiting for —Tristan suited him perfectly. Corella sounded different though. I'd never come across a living soul with that surname before. I shrugged my shoulders because I realized it didn't matter.

Now was the time to ask him if he was Tammy's friend, if he was here because she'd told him to torment me. Now was the time to confront him. He could be a little vulnerable, just as I was. But I couldn't ask. It didn't feel like the right moment. Besides, I wanted to savor this victory of mine. I would save that question for another day.

Meanwhile, I would protect my heart. I wouldn't let him sway me, and I wouldn't put myself in a position where I could be hurt. I said these things to myself yet I found my hands lifting toward him. He gave the tiniest of smiles, and the next thing I knew, his hands were in mine. There we were, standing before each other, holding hands.

"You came every day for three weeks?" I finally asked. He didn't reply, but I already knew the answer, didn't I? "How come you aren't mad at me for not showing up and making you wait so many days?"

"How can I be angry with you? I told you to take as long as you wanted. I said I'd wait for you, and I did. It's that simple."

"But…" I bit my lip. "The waiting each day. The disappointment. Wasn't that tough? I couldn't do it. And I'm sorry for what I put you through. I didn't mean to. But I couldn't come until it felt right. I had to resolve my issues." I peered up at him. "You understand, don't you?"

"I don't think there is anything to resolve between us, is there?"

I still had to ask him about Tammy, but I didn't want to discuss that now. "Now what?" I asked. "Where do we go from here?"

"Are you asking if you're my girlfriend?" he teased.

Through all this, we were still holding hands. I suddenly felt self-conscious and yanked my hands from his. What was I doing? I'd told myself I would be careful, that I wouldn't let him win me over. "That's not what I'm asking." I lifted my chin as my eyes met his. *This is insane. How can I be thinking about Tristan as my boyfriend. We just met, and I know nothing about him. This is our first real conversation.* But even as I had those thoughts, my heart cried out, this feels right! *I know it's crazy, but I must push my doubts aside. I want to enjoy this feeling and my time with Tristan, no matter where it leads.*

"Why don't we play it by ear and see how things go? If labels make you uncomfortable, don't label us," he said.

I nodded, my heart lightening. We sat on our bench (I'd started thinking of it as our bench since the first time I bumped into him here) for another hour. Or was it two? How did the time pass so quickly? We talked about everything and nothing. But too soon, it was time to go. Mom would wonder where I'd been, and she'd be worried. I'd have to think up an excuse to appease her. I wasn't quite ready to tell her or anyone else about Tristan yet. For now, he would be my secret.

CHAPTER 20

Sophie

We met the next day at our bench. "Why can't we meet at school?" I asked, my tone flippant, as though I didn't care. But the truth was, I cared. I cared a lot. "Are you afraid the crowd you hang out with will find out you are seeing me?"

"Why would you say that?" He raised an eyebrow, and I could tell he was honestly perturbed.

I gaped at him. "You really don't know? Or are you just pretending?"

He stared at me wide-eyed. "I don't know what you are talking about. Explain."

I shook my head. "Soon. Not yet."

"What about you? Have you told your friends about me?" It was his turn to question the status of our relationship.

"Not yet."

"So let this be our secret for a while," he suggested. "We

will take it slow." Then he abruptly switched subjects, catching me off-guard. "Do you like this friend of yours, Nick?"

I rolled my eyes, hiding my surprise, but I didn't pretend to misunderstand him. He didn't deserve that. I didn't even know he knew about Nick, though. Then it came to me. "Is that why you followed us to Zilker Park? To see what Nick and I were up to?" I couldn't help feeling a little miffed.

It was his turn to be appalled. "I didn't follow you. But I know you're close to Nick, so I asked. How come the two of you have never been in a relationship?"

So, Tristan wasn't at the park after all. He wasn't following me. I sighed with relief. Thank God he wasn't a psycho. Just a little too perceptive. And that wasn't a sin in my book. I frowned as I focused on answering his question about Nick. I tried to be casual about it. The truth was I would always have mixed feelings about Nick. Answering this question was difficult since Tristan was the first person who'd ever asked me about 'us.' Although everyone else seemed to insinuate that Nick and I had a relationship, they never asked outright. "It just never happened. There has always been another girl on the scene for Nick as far back as I can remember," I said, thinking about Daisy and Christina and Nick's other flirtations.

He looked thoughtful as his fingers rubbed against his chin. "I think they are all just placeholders. Nick is waiting for you. Can't you see that? And what's important is that you never said you don't like him."

"That's because I don't," I insisted.

He grunted. "Don't lie to yourself, Sophie. You just don't want to admit it because you're afraid of what would happen."

"Why are you talking about this now?" I glared at him. "Why are you pursuing my relationship with Nick when things between us are so fragile? Do you want to push me into his arms? I don't want to talk about Nick with you. It feels wrong."

"Perhaps one day it will feel right." He shrugged.

"Well, that day is not today. Topic over," I said. "Now tell me what are your thoughts on the masquerade for the homecoming dance? Were you planning on going?" I knew it would be obvious that I was desperate for a change in topic— so anxious that I was ready to bring up homecoming. Everyone knew I hated dances but perhaps Tristan wasn't aware. He claimed to know me, but how much could he really know about me?

"I thought you didn't like dances," he said.

So much for not knowing me! "I do hate dances. But this time, you are here and that changes things. I could be persuaded to go." Then it hit me. "It's in two weeks." I was being so absurd. It was too late to think about homecoming. But then the plucky side of me awakened. *Why the hell not? You won't be homecoming queen or part of the court. You are just another girl on campus. A nobody as you say. Why can't you have fun too?*

"Wasn't I supposed to have a traditional elaborate homecoming proposal planned?" His aghast expression warmed the cockles of my heart.

"Most guys do that stuff, yes." I nodded, grinning from ear to ear.

"But I don't, and I didn't. Are you disappointed? I'm sorry I'm not a very good boyfriend, am I?"

He looked so crestfallen that it broke my heart. "I'm not that kind of girl. I'm not big on such things and you're barely my boyfriend. We are just getting to know each another. So, you're off the hook. It would have probably stressed me out. Look the event is casual despite the masquerade thing. So, why don't I meet you there?"

"You don't mind going to this thing as friends?"

"Who said anything about going as friends? I'm saying I don't want the bells and the whistles. I want to keep it casual."

"That would be nice," he said. "Thank you."

"So, what do we do next?"

"Aren't you going to go dress shopping?"

"You wanna go with me?" I fluttered my eyelashes.

Seeing his horrified face, I laughed. "I will, with Shalini. But all the good stuff is probably gone by now. I've left it too late. I will see if I can raid my mom's closet and find something casual, elegant, and fun. Or I could try a thrift store and find a unique outfit."

"You know, Sophie, I think you are the coolest girl I know." He winked at me. "Nothing fazes you except the mention of Nick."

"There you go, trying to sneak his name into the conversation again," I complained.

"If you don't want to talk about him, at least tell me why you thought I didn't want to be seen with you?"

"If you'd seen me at school, you wouldn't have asked that question."

"That's not an answer, and I'm not convinced. But I am patient; I will ask you again. And next time, I won't let you avoid answering."

CHAPTER 21

Sophie

"I love our bench," Tristan said the next day when I was about to say goodbye and rush off, "but there is this little park. It's a distance away, but still on your way home. Can we meet there tomorrow?"

"That's a great idea," I said. "Why don't we walk there together after school?"

"Others might see us, so it's better this way. I will meet you there."

I nodded, but I knew that one day soon we would have to let people know about us. The more I thought about it the more I felt ready to have our relationship in the open.

The park Tristan spoke of was a pretty place. It had many paths to walk along and plenty of trees and flowers. Right in the middle, was a small pool with ducks and cute little stools strategically placed around the pond. I couldn't have thought of a more romantic place to rendezvous.

Tristan and I would hold hands and walk around the area after I dumped my bag on a stool by the pool. "Where is yours?" I asked him one day.

"I don't have one. I manage with my locker."

"That's funny. But you can always share my backpack if you have some stuff to carry."

"Tell me about this mom of yours," he said the next day. "I bet you are close."

So, I told him, adding a humorous twist. "She is a brilliant fantasy writer. If not for me, she would probably disappear into a world inhabited by the characters in her books. She loves her writing, but I'm her entire world. I'm the reason she stays here."

"Is there anything so bad about characters from books becoming a part of your life?" he teased, ruffling my hair.

"I prefer real people." Slipping my hand into his, I added, "I prefer you."

"What if I told you that I was one, too?"

"What? A character from a book?" Tilting my head to one side, I eyed him and laughed. "I would never believe you."

"I will make a note of that, madam and work on convincing you," he said, making me giggle. Since Tristan became a part of my life, I laughed and smiled more. And it wasn't just with him. It was with the others in my life, too. Mom and Shalini commented on the difference in my demeanor. Nick, I barely saw so he had little to say. And this time, it wasn't an act I was putting on for their benefit or Tristan's. I was happy. But at the back of my mind, I knew my troubles were still waiting in shadows, and the minute I forgot myself, they would return. I would never truly vanquish the demon—the incident in middle school—until I spoke about it. My silence let the demon live. But each time I thought about it, I choked up. I wondered if I could ever talk about what happened, though I thought about it all the time.

CHAPTER 22

Sophie

The next day at school, I stood frozen by my locker as I watched Tammy and the rest of her gang. They were laughing at something and it looked like they didn't have a single care in the world. They appeared to be wrapped up in a happy bubble of their own. Why was Tammy untouched by what happened? Why was I the only one left with the trauma of the eighth-grade incident? A hand on my shoulder interrupted my whorl of negativity. Without looking, I knew it was Tristan.

"You want to know what happened to me?" I said bitterly before I could stop myself. "She happened to me—Tammy Loclear." I turned toward him. He had a concerned look on his face as he looked down at me. His eyes were pools of understanding, and they helped ease the pain that was radiating in all directions from the center of my chest. He took my hand and guided me to an empty classroom.

"Tell me," he said. "Don't leave out a thing. We are running out of time."

I failed to notice his comment about time, which was my mistake. "Are you sure?" I almost sobbed. "Once I start, I don't know if I will be able to stop."

"I want to know everything." He pulled me against his chest, wrapping his arms around me.

And then I found myself telling him all about my agony. It was easier this way, speaking while being cocooned in his arms. I don't think I could have met his eyes. Seeing pity in them would have undone me. As I spoke, everything came spewing out; I hid nothing as I told him about my friendship with Tammy and her friends, how they started by patronizing me, and then the subtle bullying. I told him how they broke me down every day until there was nothing left to destroy. And finally, how they dove in for the kill. When I came to the part about the posters of me with the barely-there-clothes my voice shook. That's when I looked up at him and saw his icy rage despite his shuttered expression. He didn't say a word to me, but his arms held me tighter as though to protect me until I struggled to catch my breath. I didn't protest. It felt comforting. He seemed to be struggling to control his emotions. More than once, I felt him shudder. I felt so relieved to be able to let the words out finally. It had been so long, and I had never told anyone what happened that day. "You're the exception," I said. "I never really spoke to my mother about this. Nick told her what happened, and then she heard about it from the school. The school authorities never asked me to recount my experience; instead, they punished me for hurting Tammy. She got off scot-free without even a warning. So you see, you are the first person I am talking to about it." And then I fell silent. I was done. I'd relinquished the anguish in my soul to another's listening ear, and it was a catharsis. Remaining in his arms, I closed my eyes, finding the silence soothing.

"Did the torment end with that day?" he asked when I thought he wouldn't speak. "Did they stop? Because from your expression when you were looking at that girl, Tammy, it didn't look like she was done with torturing you."

I hesitated. I wasn't sure what to say. Should I admit that I still felt cowed when Tammy passed me in the halls, that I shrunk back into the crowd when I saw her—what would he think of me? But I decided to be truthful. I would be, even if he thought less of me because of it. "Now the taunting is more subtle. I try to ignore it. But she will never be done with me. She hates me, and you know what? I hate her too. I wish… I wish she would disappear and let me live my life." The moment I said those words, I regretted them, but it was too late to take them back. And anyway, wasn't I openly venting? Hadn't he said he wanted to know everything about what had happened to me, everything I felt? It couldn't be all good, could it? Wasn't I letting myself express what I had suppressed inside all this time? Wasn't this an opportunity for me to delve deep and admit to all that was ugly and vile within me? I peeked at him again, biting my lip. "Say something," I pleaded.

"You are the bravest girl ever." His voice sounded husky. "I'm so sorry that I wasn't there for you."

"It wasn't so bad," I admitted. "I had Nick and my mother for the most part. They helped. I wouldn't have been able to get through it without them. And talking to you today has helped. It has eased part of the ache. Thank you." And I honestly felt better. I felt like I had been locked in a tiny, dank room all this time, and the door had opened. Finally, I was out. I took a deep breath feeling free for the first time in years.

I don't know if this is the right time to ask you," he said abruptly after a while, his eyes dark with emotion, "but I have to. Why were you upset the first time I waited for you at the bench when I said I knew you?"

My heart dropped right into my stomach. How could I admit the truth after everything we'd been through in this short time? "Oh, Tristan, I'm so sorry."

"Tell me. It will be hard, but do it. I know now what you were thinking, but I want to hear it from you." A muscle worked in his jaw.

"I...assumed you were a friend of Tammy's and that... that..." My face was twisted with emotions that were as raw as night.

His arms fell to his side, and I felt empty and forlorn. His words were harsh, like an arrow that drew blood—they were bang on. "You assumed she sent me to mess with you and then make sport of you in front of the entire school? Is that what you thought?"

"I'm really sorry," I said, clinging to him. "I don't know how I could have made such a mistake." My apology was heartfelt but there was no hiding the hurt expression on his face.

"Without knowing, you assumed the worst of me."

"I'm sorry."

"I forgive you." He kissed me on my forehead, then slowly moved his lips to my cheeks, and finally when I thought I would swoon from the waiting, his lips covered mine. His actions were not seductive, but it was as if he was trying to tell me something without saying a word. His lips lingered on mine, and then I kissed him back with everything I had. My heart cried out while I kissed him, because I sensed what he'd left unsaid—this was goodbye. We would never have another moment on our bench. We would never share another kiss. I was losing him. Our kiss went on for what seemed like forever. Was it just one kiss or were many tied together so closely that it felt like one? I didn't know and I couldn't think. I didn't want to think; I just wanted this feeling to continue without words. I knew if he spoke, he'd say the actual words to me, but if we kept kissing, he wouldn't leave me— he couldn't go away.

When he broke away, I was sobbing. "Don't cry," he said. "You knew from the first time we met that this was momentary. That I would go away."

"I didn't," I said. "I thought we would be forever. Why do you have to go? Is it because you are angry with me?" But even as I said the words, I knew deep inside what I'd always known, that he would say adieu one day and leave a hole in my heart. Had he been here only to help me talk about Tammy and the bullying? Isn't that why he said we were running out of time? Isn't that why he spoke about Nick? Because he knew I would need someone to lean on when he was gone?

"Don't let her win," he said. "Live your life the way you want to. Love who you want to. You will soon be free of her."

"I love you," I cried out.

"You don't. You only think you do. Look inside and you will know who you have loved all this time."

"What about the dance?" I asked, desperate to compel him to stay.

"Go with Nick," he replied.

And then he was gone. I sobbed, wrapping my arms around myself, completing the embrace Tristan had broken—alone and adrift, knowing deep down that without him I wouldn't be the same.

CHAPTER 23

Sophie

I was slowly falling apart, and nothing could stop it. I knew it, but it would be a while before the cracks would show to those around me, at least those who still cared. To many, I never really mattered.

It was a few more days until homecoming. On the day of the football game, they would crown the Homecoming King and Queen and announce the rest of their court at halftime. School spirit required that I attend. I knew it would mean a lot to Nick, but I couldn't go. Besides, I had an awful feeling that Nick and Christina would be king and queen. This was not something I wanted to see first-hand. I'd hear about it from Shalini, definitely not from Nick himself. He was not the sort to brag. He would have to go with Christina to this dance. I couldn't let it affect me. Here I was, heartbroken about Tristan, but thoughts of Nick still affected me.

I decided to confess secrets of my own and told Shalini

about Tristan. I expected surprise, happiness, and then sorrow for my loss, but all I got was disbelief. From her facial expression, I could tell she thought I'd made him up because I couldn't get over Nick. "How can you not believe me?"

"I do. Who says I don't?" She sounded defensive.

"Your expression tells me you don't." I jabbed a finger toward her chest. "He came to this school, or rather he used to. I don't know which class he was in, but he was a student here."

"And he left school because he broke up with you?" She stared at me with rounded eyes. "Why did I never see him with you?"

"Because we were careful. We didn't want anyone to know about us until we were ready." Why was she making me feel so defensive? He was real. I knew he was. To my ears, my voice sounded freezing when I said, "I don't know why he left or why he had to go but he did. And you know what, before he left, I talked to him about Tammy. It was the first time I talked to anyone about her; he made me feel better. He promised me I would be free of her."

"You don't appear to be better." She wrinkled her nose.

"That's because I'm upset about him leaving. My heart is breaking."

My despair made Shalini realize I was on the brink of a disaster, and she decided to tiptoe around me. "Okay, I believe you. I'm sorry. I'm sorry."

This is what I needed—a sympathetic friend to make

things better even though I knew they would never be better. "What am I supposed to do without him?"

Her response was not as kind as I expected, but perhaps, she thought I needed a dose of strong medicine. "You go on. What else can you do? You are too young to cry over a boy you knew for a few days. You will find another one. I'm sure you will. You never thought you would meet Tristan, but you did. Give it time."

"I don't want to meet anyone else." I glared at her, my jaw tight. "There can be nobody like Tristan. I love him and will wait for him as long as it takes."

"If that's what you want to do, that's fine." Shalini patted my arm. She was a girl with infinite patience, and it didn't matter that I was testing her. She would be there for me.

"Will you tell me about the match and the dance?" I asked, trying hard to make a show of being excited, to show her I was okay.

Shalini's face fell. "Won't you come? You were so excited about homecoming."

"I can't. I just can't. My excitement was all because of Tristan. If he isn't here there is no point in my going. But if you tell me everything, it will be almost like me being there."

"Does this mean that you are going to be melancholy again?" She bit her lip, studying me. "I love you as you are— happy or sad— but seeing you these past days, I realized the way you lit up from inside made me very happy."

"It was all on account of Tristan." I shook my head. "But I will be fine. I need time to grieve. And then I will be okay."

I told Mom I was sick. She was so concerned that I felt terrible about lying to her. She believed me because I looked ill. I was so pale that she wanted to rush me to the doctor, but I told her all I needed was a few days' rest. Missing home-coming and all the events would allow me a chance to feel better.

"But don't you want to go to the dance if not the match?"

"When do I ever go to dances?"

"I thought this time… Nick would ask you and you would go."

I laughed lightly. "Nick never asked me, poor guy. I warned him against it years ago. He has never asked again."

"Oh! I'm sorry I mentioned it." Mom was so remorseful that I felt terrible all over again.

CHAPTER 24

Sophie

The night of the homecoming dance, the call came from Shalini and Nick. They were frantic. When she heard the news, I sensed Mom's relief that I hadn't gone to the dance. Something unexpected had happened—they found Tammy at the bottom of the stairs of a passage outside the gym where the dance was being held. The steps were steep, and they thought she lost her balance because of her heels and fell down the steps. She was dead on impact. Everybody was in shock and was mourning her loss. A candlelight vigil was planned on the school grounds for the following evening.

I felt frozen.

"Oh, that poor girl," my mother kept saying.

I wanted to scream at her and say—what about me? What about what Tammy had been doing to me? I was miserable because of her. Now I'm finally free. I knew this was not the right thing to feel and that I should be sorry. I should be sad.

We'd lost a classmate. Someone so young with their whole life ahead of them. But I didn't feel any of those things. I stared at my mom as she wept tears for the girl I hated most in life and death, and in that moment, I almost hated my mom too.

Then as if someone had poured ice-water down my back, Tristan's words came back to me — *live your life the way you want to. Love who you want to. You will soon be free of her.* And now I was free of her. Just like that. Was this his idea of a parting gift to me? I was horrified. I had to tell my mom about this. The thought that Tristan would have taken a life to protect me, to avenge me, was dismaying.

"Mom, I have a secret I must tell you."

"Right now, sweetheart?" She paled and covered her mouth with one hand. "Is this about Tammy?"

"Not exactly but she is a part of it." And then I told her about Tristan. I told her everything. About the first time I saw him, the first time we met, about the bench and the park, the kiss, our talk about Tammy—all of it. I watched the blood drain from my mother's face as I spilled my guts about Tristan.

"Why are you telling me this now?" Mom's voice sounded strangled, as though she had to force the words from her now bloodless lips.

"Because… because I think… I think that it was Tristan who killed Tammy. Before he left, he told me I would be free of her. Mom, I love him so much, and don't want him to get into trouble. Mom, please don't tell the cops about him.

Shalini says they think it was an accident. Please let them think that. I just…" Pausing, I swallowed hard before continuing. "I just had to talk to someone and share my fears, and I couldn't tell Shalini because she didn't believe Tristan was real. She thinks I made him up. But I don't have such a wild imagination. I could never do it. He is real, Mom, and I think he killed Tammy."

Mom grasped my hands in a deathlike grip, hers trembling. She kissed my hands and looked at me, tears flooding her eyes. "You don't have a wild imagination, honey. But… I… I do. Tristan. Tristan is a boy." A soft moan escaped her, and she swallowed hard. "But he is a boy I made up. You… you must have read my manuscript."

I recoiled from her as though she had struck me. "What are you saying? You knew about Tristan? You sent him?"

"That's not what I'm saying. I'm saying he is make-believe. He is a character I wrote about for you—just for you —to make myself feel a little better about what was happening in your life. Listen to me, I made him up. I never meant for you to read about him but you must have found the book."

"Why are you lying? Please stop." I covered my ears. I refused to hear more of her nonsense. Tristan was real. Perhaps he didn't kill Tammy. I hope he hadn't, but he was real.

Mom didn't reply. Instead, she ran from the room and returned with a book. It was one of those long notepads in which she made her writing notes. It looked familiar. I could almost visualize myself sitting in the dark, poring over its pages, with only a bedside lamp to give me light. But I shook my head. It wasn't true.

"Look at this." She pushed the pad into my hands. "Read it."

"I won't." I clenched my hands into fists and stepped back, letting the book fall to the ground like the devil incarnate.

But Mom wasn't having any of it. She picked up the book and forcibly put it back in my hand, murmuring—*what have I done?* She looked frantic, and that's the only reason I gave in and opened the book, deciding to glance at a few pages to satisfy her. It was a big mistake. I was better off never opening it. The things I told my mom moments ago jumped out at me from the pages—the bench, the park, the secret meetings, the name Tristan, and even our kiss. It was all there, my life in its pages. I'd just told her about it. How could she have written it down? I felt hollowed from the inside out. This couldn't be happening. Maybe she'd been spying on me? Following me and then writing everything down? Perhaps she'd written about my life because she hadn't been writing recently and my life sounded interesting?

"Even if this were true and I'm not saying I believe you, why would you do this? Why would you write about my life?"

"I wanted to feel better and feel more in control. And I wanted to help you, give you a friend, but I didn't dare to tell you I wrote you a story. I thought it would be my secret."

So, my mom had secrets too! I heard her words, but I still couldn't accept it. There had to be an explanation. But as I looked at her face, I saw the truth. But knowing the truth and accepting reality are different things; I wouldn't accept it. *I couldn't.*

"Corella is an anagram of Loclear, Tammy's surname," Mom whispered.

"What?"

"I wanted the one who healed you in my musings to be Tammy's opposite —Tristan. But everything was linked to her. That's why I chose an anagram."

Even as the truth of what happened set in, my thoughts rushed to fill the void. —thoughts of Tristan. Tristan was real. He would always be real to me. I smiled at my mother. "This is a delightful story. I enjoyed reading it. But I know my Tristan is real. Your story is a coincidence. He is gone now, but will return for me one day. And I am going to wait for him."

I believe that was when I slipped into a world of my own. I refused to hear my mother pleading that Tristan was fictional or rather, I heard but ignored her and receded into a world where Tristan existed or at least one where I was waiting for him to return to me. It felt wonderful, and I never wanted to leave that place. Soon, Tristan would return, and I could speak to and hug him, and nothing would keep us apart. We would be together forever.

My mother tried hard to pull me back. After failing on her own, she took me to a renowned psychologist. When all I did was chat about Tristan or remain stubbornly silent with my hands crossed, the psychologist washed his hands of me. He believed that my low self-esteem had led me to this delusional state. Mom didn't like what she heard and slightly changed tactics by taking me to a psychiatrist. But she couldn't help either. I'd receded too far into my own world. My distressed mother did everything she could, but how could she succeed when I didn't want her to win? Her winning would mean that I lost Tristan. I couldn't allow that, could I? School, grades, and friends meant nothing to me anymore and try as I did, I couldn't care about them. Mom lost me; her world lost me.

Epilogue

SOPHIE

This mental health facility is my home now. I will not argue with the semantics. You can call it a psychiatric facility or an asylum. But it's not one of those horrible places that locks people up and drugs them until they go mad. It's a gentle place where the staff genuinely care about us. They are non-confrontational and calm. They express their opinions as concern rather than judgment. All the credit goes to my mother for finding this place. God bless her!

Mama comes to see me every day. Since I've been here, I've reverted to my childhood name for her. Somehow, it feels comforting. I think she likes it, too. She seems fragile—a mere shadow of the woman she used to be. I feel it's my fault that I've done this to her, or—did she do this to herself? After all, it was her idea to write about Tristan. Occasionally, she brings a few sheets of paper with her. I can tell what it is—a new story for me to read. But all she does is fidget with the documents in her hands, almost crumpling them to bits. She never ends up giving them to me. I think she is afraid of what else could go wrong. What would happen if I snatched the pages from her and either read them or tore them to pieces? I don't know. I see myself going either way. But I could never be so cruel to my beloved mother. Whatever she does with those papers, must be her choice. I think it's too late, anyway. No words can help me now.

Mama talks, and sometimes I talk back. Often, I can see hope in her eyes—hope that I will be okay, but whenever I bring up Tristan, she becomes distressed. In the end, she walks away with her shoulders dropping. I shouldn't talk about him to her, but I love him. I can't help it. She doesn't stay gone for long. She will be back again. Tomorrow is another day. I'm her daughter and she will never give up on me. That's what a good parent does, and Mama is the best. She has always put me first.

I always knew I was her entire world. But who knew that instead of her being the one to live in a world of characters from books like she always talked about, it would be me? Who knew I would love it too? But having said that, I know I'm getting better, or at least I'm getting better at pretending to get better. And it is because of Nick. He comes to see me, too. And every time he is near Tristan slips away. Nick and I have animated conversations, and we talk about chess and the video games we used to play. It's a lot of fun. And one more big thing—Nick confessed that he loves me. I was over the moon. The dolt—why did he take so long? Why did he wait for me to go mad before confessing his feelings? He told me he stopped seeing Christina. He says that one day I can leave this place, and then we can start our lives together. I hope his words are true because I would love to have a life with Nick.

But when Nick leaves, Tristan returns, and I always welcome him with open arms. I can't seem to stay away from him. We have our little life together, too. When I walk in the garden, he is with me. He is with me when I'm watching television, and when I sleep, he lays down beside me, sleeping too. Sometimes, if he is very restless, he sits in the chair watching me sleep. I feel safe with him. He only leaves when I want him to. And I mostly never want him to go. I like having him around.

However, when I have my chats with the doctors about my mental well-being Tristan insists on leaving. He says I shouldn't talk to them about him; otherwise, they will never let me leave. He is right. My Tristan is so wise.

Shalini never comes to see me. What happened to me was too much for her to bear. It's okay. I'm used to losing friends and have my memories of her.

Tristan and I share a secret. It took me a while to remember. Going crazy can get in the way, you see, but when I remembered, I told Tristan. I knew he would never tell—he loves me, after all. Tristan never killed Tammy. But Tammy's death wasn't an accident either. Because you see, I killed her. I don't know if I meant to. But it happened.

On the night of the dance, I kept thinking about Tristan, and how he told me I was free of Tammy. The desire to confront her became so strong that I snuck out of the house and hid at school where I knew Tammy was bound to pass by. The homecoming dance was a masquerade, so I wore a mask so that even if anyone saw me, they wouldn't recognize me.

I'd spent so many years staring at Tammy, hating her that I knew this girl so well. Better than her own mother, many would say. I knew all her dirty little secrets and habits. After all, I'd learned long ago that every monster has a weakness. None are indestructible. I just had to persist until I vanquished them. Then they had to go away. See, I told my mother that video games would help.

I waited till Tammy was alone and when she started climbing the stairs to have a drink on the sly from a little metal flask hidden in her purse, I emerged from my hiding place and removed my mask. Tammy was initially shocked to see me but then she recovered and had plenty of acidic comments to make. I couldn't take it anymore. I pushed her, channeling all the anger I had toward her. She looked at me in shock and then she was toppling backward. I don't know what I wanted—whether to hurt her or kill her. But kill her, I did. I stood at the top of the stairs staring down at her broken body, then I put my mask back on and went home. My body was shaking but my mind was blank. I couldn't feel anything —no fear, regret or even euphoria.

I snuck back home to bed and my mother was none the

wiser that I'd been out. For a long time, I waited for the cops to come for me, but nobody came. Hours passed and then came the news from Shalini and Nick—Tammy was dead. That's when I forgot that I had killed her. I believed I'd been sick at home. And no one questioned me. No one suspected a thing even though Tammy and I were mortal enemies because in their eyes, I was a pathetic little fool incapable of murder. Everyone believed that I was lying sick in bed at home or, in Shalini's case moping about a make-believe boyfriend. I played things out so well that for a long time even I believed that Tammy's death was an accident. It is only now that I have time to think that the events of that night have come back to me. Her death is a secret that now lives with Tristan and me. Both of us will never tell.

Now you know too. But you will never tell, will you?

The End

Hope

SHIKA DESOUZA

There's something which lights up the universe like a single firework in the dark night sky, like the end to every tunnel or the hug that makes everything alright.

Hope is that thing, that feeling, the last item let out into the world from Pandora's mystical box.

Oh, Hope is like a little cute child who encourages you, adores you and at times even enlightens you. She is the one who wraps you in her warmth when your day feels like it had an apocalyptic end.

She always glides beside you never letting you go across the line toward evil, insanity and utter darkness.

There are times when your pain feels unbearable, your thirst unquenchable but Hope is like the coat which always fits, the ever-faithful dog who continues to wait at the station even after his master's tragic death and the tea light floating in the depths of the murky chilly and misty lake.

When despair like the stalker he is, knocks at your door, Hope is the kind loving friend who opens it with you.

Hope will give us the calmness and the strength to escape from the anxiety of depression, we have been locked in by no one but ourselves.

Hope, to put it bluntly is there when problems find you, entrap you and surround you with their horrible lies.

Dear Reader

If you liked this book and it made an impression, I ask you to leave a review minus spoilers. *And Then You Were Gone* is on Goodreads and Amazon. A review makes a significant difference to a writer, and I would greatly appreciate yours, even if it is only a few lines. Thank you so much for reading.

Credits

Editors : Barbara Daniels Dena and Caron Pescatore

Developmental Editor : Alexander Way-B

Proof Reading : Daisy B

Cover Art : Mario Teodosio

Cover Design : Ideascope (Vishvesh Desai, Dhruv C and Tanya Singhania)

Book Design : Suzanne Minae

Poems : Ira Rana and Shika Desouza

Acknowledgments

This book wouldn't have been possible without Neeti Saraf Agarwal. My oldest friend and my source of research for all things high school and Austin. Thank you, Neeti. Alexander Way- B and Daisy B thank you for nudging me gently when I faltered. Thank you, dear Kelly Miller, for all your insightful and introspective observations and questions. It made a big difference. I appreciate your and Joy York's wonderful contributions to the blurb. Thank you, Anna Casamento Arrigo and Danie Takeshita, for your early comments. Thank you, Angela McPherson, Daisy Wood, Eve Koguce, Joy York, and Lynda Renham, for reading and for your developmental comments and encouraging feed-back. Each of you contributed a perspective that influenced the book. Barbara, thank you for working on this book despite your loss of Zoe. Ira, I loved your poem, 'Walls.' It spoke to me as soon as I read it. It perfectly represented what Sophie was going through. Thank you to Ian, my dearest husband for reminding me to write daily. Your reassurances helped me tremendously at a time when I was facing writer's block. Thank you for being my support-system. Shika, my lovely girl, thanks for allowing me to use your favorite name, the name you wish you had been born with—Sophie. I didn't name you Sophie, but I wrote you a book with a character called Sophie. I loved your poem 'Hope' so much. Thank you for letting me include it in the book. I think in the end, hope is what Sophie needs the most. Neil, my sensitive, sweet son, thank you for always inspiring me to write. And thanks to the lovely stranger on the plane who heard the synopsis of *And Then You Were Gone* and made insightful suggestions even before I started writing. And last but not the least my gratitude to the readers of *And Then You Were Gone*.

Also by Ivy Logan

THE BREACH CHRONICLES

ORIGINS

The Legend of Ava

(A Short Story)

BOOK I - BROKEN

Broken But Not Lost

BOOK II - METAMORPHOSIS

The Girl With No Face

BOOK III - REDEMPTION

The Quest from Vengeance to Redemption

The Breach Chronicles

PREQUEL

ORIGINS - THE LEGEND OF AVA

(A Short Story)

Ava

She travels to the future. That is her cross to bear. She is forbidden
to interfere in the cataclysmic events she witnesses, even if her
heart tells her otherwise. But this time, she has seen too much
bloodshed. Two innocents will die, and their deaths will alter the
future of the supernaturals forever. What should Ava do? Should
she intervene and try to change the future? Or should she follow
the rules and let things unfold as predetermined?

Selena

All she wanted was to help her friend. She did not know then what
the consequences would be. Now it is too late. Will she gamble her
life to save the one she loves?

Tagasaya

They say he is a beast; they treat him like a monster—even though
he doesn't feel like one. But now they have taken everything from
him, and his heart cries for vengeance. Will he accept the monster
inside to claim his revenge?

*A time-traveling sorceress. Star-crossed lovers. Monsters with a
conscience.*

Things spiral out of control when they all come together. Read *The Prequel to The Breach Chronicles; Origins*, as it sets the stage for a conflict between two worlds and their inhabitants. Supernaturals on one side and humans on the other. Walking a thin line between the two worlds are the Guardian sorceresses.

These are their stories.

The Breach Chronicles

BOOK I

BROKEN BUT NOT LOST

A Young Adult Fantasy & Romance Adventure

It all began with a prophecy

Sorceress Caitlin believed she could fight it

But then, love came calling, and all was lost

Her daughter, a half-blood sorceress, Talia, had a unique childhood

Bereft of dolls, but not of love

Taught to protect herself

Trained to escape detection

Schooled to face an unknown menace

When her family's worst nightmare comes to pass

Talia finds her sheltered life spinning out of control

Everything she believes in

Everyone she loves

Are cruelly snatched away

She must flee the attentions of a mad king

Denied her supernatural legacy

She chooses the path of retribution

But sometimes, we are worthy of love

Even if we do not seek it

The Breach Chronicles

BOOK II

METAMORPHOSIS

The Girl With No Face

A Young Adult

Romance & Contemporary Fantasy

Amidst the luminescence and incandescent beauty of the rare pink diamonds of Peradora, South America, lives Amelia, a teen oblivious to her supernatural bloodline. It would appear that she has the perfect life.

Until it turns out, her entire life is a lie

Forced to confront secrets from her past

Amelia must distinguish between the truth and lies in her brutal fight against the Peradorian dictator, her own uncle.

Her metamorphosis becomes the clarion call of a revolution

While matters of the heart complicate her life further

Will she ever get over her first love, Adrian whose adventurous spirit made her feel alive? Is Noah, the handsome bodyguard she can't seem to ignore, a friend, foe, or much more than that?

Both Noah and Adrian are hiding secrets of their own

Will their secrets destroy Amelia?

As she takes on the fight of her life, Amelia will soon learn that some secrets are best buried in the past, and some truths can set you free.

And in the end: She is the girl with no face

Will she find herself again?

The Breach Chronicles

BOOK III

REDEMPTION

A Quest: From Vengeance to Redemption

A Young Adult Contemporary Fantasy

AMELIA

She took on the mighty Peradorian dictator and lost. She loved Noah, but she might never see him again. Now she and Adrian are on the run. To make things worse, her shapeshifting ability has deserted her. What lies ahead?

NOAH

He accepted that he was a monster to save the girl he loved, even if it meant losing her. The Heichi queen is determined to kill him and protect her throne at all costs. Now a sorceress has predicted great darkness in Amelia's future. Will he be able to save her?

ADRIAN

He chose Amelia over his freedom and family. He protected her at all costs. Why does her heart still belong to another?

It's all coming together in the exciting finale of *The Breach Chronicles—Redemption*. New enemies will rise, and old friends will rush to the rescue. Secrets will be revealed. Promises will be made and promises will be broken. The lines will blur between friend and foe. Everyone is in a race against time, fighting for their life. But will they find Redemption?

About the Author

Ivy is passionate about stories, both writing and reading them. Her stories often blend fractured fairy tales and dark fantasy but are always full of love and light. She can't always promise you'll find the ending you're looking for.

Ivy adores writing about strong women and girls who are far from perfect. Her characters are fighters, but they love, cry, hurt, and bleed. They believe in family, friendship, and sacrifice. They are authentic, fragile and vulnerable, while being strong as you and I. And Then You Were Gone is her first foray into contemporary women's fiction.

On Facebook and Twitter (X), Ivy is a big supporter of books based on strong women real and fictional and she is a huge cheerleader of the writing community. You can find her at @Ivyloganauthor on X and Facebook at https://www.facebook.com/ivyloganauthor. You can also follow her on Blue Sky at @ivylogan.bsky.social.

Reviews

Origins

I enjoyed this, it's the first title I've read by Ivy Logan and she shows a lot of promise as an author. I understand this is a prequel to a series, so I will certainly be checking out the other titles in the series. This is a short title but that is reflected in the price. Highly recommended.

Broken

I find it amazing when someone can world build and create a credible and engaging story simultaneously. Ivy Logan does this masterfully. She has created a story full of adversity, sacrifice and love while creating two worlds one of them supernatural and another more earthbound. Weaving the two together Ivy makes a powerful story that flows across the pages pulling you in. It is a unique experience that hollows out a place in your heart for Talia, you feel her highs and lows exponentially. I highly recommend that you follow Talia's story. Kudos to Ivy Logan for crafting such a story.

Redemption

I have enjoyed every book in this complex, intricately woven young adult fantasy tale of The Breach Chronicles. Redemption is totally captivating and a perfect end to this dynamic series. I was first attracted to the series because of the strong female characters which have remained consistent throughout the series. Too often strong female characters are portrayed as abrasive or flawless superheroes. Not true in this story. The female protagonists are independent but with a dose of vulnerability. They are loyal, determined, and are willing to make the hard choices regardless of the danger to themselves.

The plots between these books are all so expertly crafted and intertwined, with well-developed characters that constantly surprised and amazed me. The multilayered themes go beyond good and evil to social injustice, revenge, jealousy, power, greed, friendship, and love. Logan is a masterful storyteller. I am amazed at the complexity of these stories filled with twists, turns, and a-ha moments. The pace remained brisk with something new to capture my attention with each turn of the page. I highly recommend this amazing fantasy series. I look forward to reading more from Ivy Logan.

Metamorphosis

This wonderfully written tale of love, betrayal, magic, fate, revenge, and acceptance caught me from the very first page and NEVER let go! In part, it reminded me of a few

Shakespearean plays (Henry V, Richard the III, Hamlet, Macbeth, -some evil is definitely afoot-no spoilers here-A Midsummer's Night Dream-and a hint of Romeo and Juliet). Amelia, our protagonist has a great deal to handle. From freeing Peradora from her own uncle's grips, to accepting her fated bloodline, and deciding who her true love might be-

There is so much action, fantasy, twists and turns that I was absolutely vested in each word. The characters are beautifully written. The dialogue superb. Most highly recommended! (I anticipated Metamorphosis in paperback before the holidays to gift to three of my grandchildren!)

Broken

The book gripped me from the beginning. It carried me through the challenges of these women who have to fight for everything. The story made me smile, cry and laugh. I like the idea of the connection of between the animals and the sorceresses. For me it a fairytale with mix with magic and love. Ivy writes a heart-wrenching story of love, adventure and sacrifice. The write has a fantastic imagination, and weaves together a beautiful story, which will keep you wanting for more.

Metamorphosis

Ivy Logan's second book of the Breach Chronicles - 'Metamorphosis', far exceeded my expectations. "For what is

a heart if not an instrument of torture? It allows you to love, and then it snatches it all away. A fleeting moment of happiness in the vast abyss of time, that's what it allows you." Copy write: Ivy Logan, Metamorphosis.

It is a story of heartbreak, sacrifice, love and loss; one that captures your heart, and ensnares your soul. Running parallel to all of these things, is faith, as this instils within all of us, the hope, that by revealing our true self to the world, it will not elicit the pain of rejection.

Metamorphosis

Metamorphosis, is a carefully and intricately woven book, that pulls you in all directions, leading you down paths that you would never have expected. Ivy Logan has surpassed all expectations with this new book, she is a beautiful weaver of words, and a master of building secrets, amidst intrigue, keeping the reader captivated at all times. The book is set in the present day, but the long distant past of another realm holds all the secrets.

It is a beautiful book, a MUST read!!

Origins

And now I really do have to wait for book two in the Breach Chronicles. I read book one, and it was phenomenal! The story was gripping and the characters endearing--except the evil ones, of course. But I fell in love with Ava, who featured in that story, and wanted to know more about her. So, I was happy to find this prequel novella.

The problem is that it's not nearly enough! 😞😞 This short story gives more detail for the backdrop of book one in the series, Broken. FYI that book can be read as a standalone; it does not end in a cliffhanger. So, there is no need to wait for book two to be released before reading it. As for me, I now must wait for book 2. 😭😭😭 Enjoy!!!

Redemption

Having read the Breach Chronicles, what I anticipated, as this fantastic journey continued, is not what I thought. It is in keeping with the themes of love, animosity, courage, friendships, and overcoming the varied obstacles in the path to finding justice. Friendships, once strong and cherished are tested-it is here that an aha moment of truth, acceptance, and self-awareness comes to the surface. The battles brilliantly unfolded and the cause and effects, with their myriad of foils and victories reveal themselves! Our heroine had opened that proverbial 'Pandora's' box and its contents yielded battles to be fought-friendships broken-but, still endurance and courage prevail! There is something extraordinarily beautiful and inspiring about an author's ability to weave such cohesive and fantastic tales. Redemption goes above the fantastic. Each character with their strengths and flaws is captivating and one can easily envision them in whole and part. They are that well developed! I remember meeting Ava in Origins and was drawn in and eager to discover more. In the end and many journeys hence, it is Amelia who begs my full attention. A page turning feast for every sense. Expect the unexpected (especially if you've already read the series). I am so extremely eager what Author Logan comes up with next! This book is worthy of greater than 5 ☆!

Metamorphosis

As Logan's readers have come to expect, Metamorphosis is full of memorable characters. Amelia is a highly believable young woman, prone to mistakes, misinterpretations, emotional turmoil, angst, and anger. Her uncle, Liam, is more shallow and a lot more dangerous than she realizes. But both of Amelia's love interests, Adrian and Noah, are just as full of surprises and secrets as she is. We get to know the key characters because Logan gives each of them several point-of-view chapters. This technique works on several levels. On the one hand, we get to see feelings and concerns that aren't revealed to the other characters. These POV shifts also put us more squarely in the action of the novel.

I highly recommend Metamorphosis, even for readers who eschew fantasy tales. Ivy Logan will change your mind.

Broken

This is a beautifully told, well-written, gripping fantasy about love, family, found family, good vs. evil, and self-sacrifice. I enjoyed the writing style, pacing, and uniqueness of the story. The author built fascinating worlds and the characters were well developed and relatable. I especially loved Caitlin and Talia—two captivating, skillful, and powerful female characters. If you enjoy young adult fantasy with excellent world building, an exciting storyline, and strong, passionate female characters this book is for you.

Redemption

"REDEMPTION" is the third book of Ivy Logan's trilogy, "The Breach Chronicles", a beautifully written magical saga full of unexpected twists and turns. It's a gripping and page turning story where there is no single dull moment; quite the contrary! You're caught up in a flurry of events, a war between good end evil, darkness and redemption, magical creatures and humans.

Broken

Broken (The Breach Chronicles -Book 1) by Ivy Logan is an epic, YA fantasy with a female POV. As in the struggle between family legacy, finding the strength to forge your own path and the ability to manage and decipher what must be accomplished... and when. The world the author created is mysterious and feels mystical and otherworldly from the beginning. The vivid scene of a new sorceress being born and the ancient wraiths speaking in cryptic messages was mesmerizing. Loved it! The relatable themes of love, betrayal, power vs. control and choice all come together across time with a young Caitlin making choices that could destroy everything her mother worked for.

A battle with a dragon and a fiercely independent sorceress. Yes, please!

Although the plot felt slightly overwritten in the last few chapters, I was thrilled to read a YA book that I can wholeheartedly recommend to young people that keeps in tune with a more reader-friendly style of writing.

Rather than capitalizing on extreme violence or the sexualization of teenagers found in some YA, this tale takes the high road and focuses its light on the heroines journey, sacrifice for future generations, family and what love looks like when its given away and what true love is when it returns home again.

Metamorphosis

Metamorphosis is set in a kind of parallel universe to the one we're used to. We experience magic, mysticism, and fantasy, which are clearly not of our world, but it all takes place in the 21st Century, with its obsession with media overload and celebrity worship. This is not a combination that lends itself easily to an entertaining novel, but Logan makes it all work seamlessly.

Metamorphosis

The story of Amelia Diaz's struggle to survive her "gilded cage" environment and to make a difference in the lives of the people of Peradora, the fictitious South American country over which her uncle, Liam, rules with an iron fist and a cold heart. The plot is complex, as it merges fantasy, adventure, mystery, thriller, and romance in this coming-of-age tale of a beautiful young girl who struggles to understand the reality of her world and to find her true self along the way. Neither is an easy quest.

Origins

I read Origins: The Legend of Ava (The Breach Chronicles) by Ivy Logan while returning from a brief vacation. The book is short at forty-five pages, so I got through it in no time. I have already read Broken book one, and it is an amazing novel. The characters Logan has created are rich, kind, compassionate, and brave. Ava is a wonderful example to young adults, with her unquestionable loyalty and a heart to step in and save others who are in need and troubled. Even though Ava is given strict orders not to intervene, her heart is bigger than her reasoning. Logan also shows there are conse-quences when interfering in things we should not. This prequel is a great lead into book two. If you've not read Broken, I highly recommend you do. Logan is an excellent storyteller and draws you into the world she has created. 5 brilliant stars.

Metamorphosis

Metamorphosis is the second book in Ivy Logan's Breach Chronicles young adult fantasy series., The novel is an exciting, compelling read. This comes from someone who normally avoids both YA and fantasy. But I enjoyed Broken, the first book in Logan's series, so I already knew her work and her knack for pulling the reader into the middle of the story and never letting go.

Metamorphosis

'Metamorphosis' is the second narrative in The Breach Chronicles, but can be read as a standalone. I loved 'Broken', but I love Metamorphosis more! Amelia is a fragile, heart-broken young girl, who goes through so much horror at the hand of her uncle, a vicious, lying, scheming dictator, whose lust for wealth dominates everything. I love Amelia's growth throughout the book. She's flawed and sincere, continually challenging herself and believing she is a coward; not deserving of respect or love. The love interests—oh, my heart—are splendidly done. First Adrian, later Noah. I think I fell in love a little with Noah. Both Amelia and Noah have secrets—big secrets—which are revealed as the book goes on. The world-building is nicely done, and the twists and turns ensure the story cracks along at a good pace. The fantasy element weaves delightfully with this sweet coming of age tale. I read Metamorphosis in two sittings, wishing to know how the story would play out. And the ending?... Left me craving more. I'm desperate to see where this story goes. I very much recommend this well written, YA Fantasy, coming of age novel. Well done Ms Logan.

Broken

A prince, a dragon, a fearless warrior named Talia- what more could you want from a book? *Broken* by Ivy Logan is one of those books you can't put down. An exceptional story with exceptional characters that, you grow to love and root for. I also love happy endings, thank you, Ivy Logan.

At first, I found it hard to connect with the story but after reading through a few pages, I was hooked. The main character, Talia is a fierce warrior who puts family above all else. "Talia has always put her family before herself, no sacrifice too great." This line in the book describes Talia perfectly. She is loyal, selfless, and determined. A true heroine. I highly recommend this love story for any age. It will inspire all generations, from young to old, to believe they can overcome great obstacles in life if they stand strong and firm in their convictions. Talia is a wonderful example of what happens when perseverance and love rise to the challenge of any situation. Love conquers all. 5 heartwarming stars for *Broken*. Good job, Ivy Logan.

Excerpt from Origins
THE LEGEND OF AVA

THE DYING – AVA

Ava watched the hysterical girl dart in and out of the gloomy shadows cast by the dense trees that loomed in her path. She was the very personification of fear. Ava could almost see the dark, poisonous cloud of overwhelming distress hovering over her. An invisible thread must bind them both together, because Ava felt the cold fingers of dread reach within her. It wrapped itself around her heart, constricting and squeezing. Breathless, she balled the fingers of her left hand into a tight fist. Her nails bit into the soft skin of her palm, drawing blood, but the pain failed to distract her. She felt the fear burning through her skin, seeping into every pore of her body.

Stay silent, stay hidden, and never let the ones you watch, spot you, she reminded herself. But the overwhelming anxiety she felt for the girl made her reckless. The girl was a stranger to her but that didn't make her life any less valuable. She had to stop her. She couldn't stay silent any longer. Ignoring all her instincts, she called out a warning, "Stop! Don't go that way!" Oblivious to her frantic plea, the girl quickened her pace. *She can't hear me*, Ava realized. When she moved through time, only humans naturally attuned to the supernatural sensed her. The girl was not one of them. *What was about to happen?*

～

Nia had stolen away to meet a boy.

Jai was wild, worldly-wise and everything her father hated. Which made him just right for her. The forest on the outskirts of their town, dark and mysterious, seemed like the perfect place for an assignation, the perfect place to infuse the right dose of mystery and romance into their budding relationship. She was a diehard romantic after all. She didn't know then, what this rendezvous would cost her.

In the fading twilight the forest didn't look so inviting and exotic anymore. It was downright forbidding. Fear began to prey on her mind. *Why had she asked Jai to meet her in such a secluded setting? Would he be waiting for her or would he be late?*

She remembered his reaction. He had initially cringed at the thought of the meeting in the forest, but had given in. All the men in her life eventually caved in. The combined force of her charm and persuasive abilities became too much for them to withstand. Their outright 'No' became a 'Maybe' and then finally a reluctant 'Yes'. Victims of her manipulation always made the mistake of underestimating her. They thought she was as easy-going. They thought they were the ones manipulating her. They were wrong. On the outside, she seemed soft, feminine, and helpless. But she used her softness as a tool to mold people to her way of thinking. The truth was she was hard and determined.

Jai was a different matter. There was nothing soft about him. He was outrageous and like a rough-cut diamond. His wild reputation provoked the protective instincts of her brothers towards her. "*No,* you can't have him. He was not a suitable choice," they said. Little had they known that their rejection only made Jai seem even more attractive. She had always been attracted to bad boys, a *taboo* bad boy, was even more appealing. The recklessness of such situations made her feel like a rebel.

But there in the stifling forest, she didn't feel rebellious anymore, only desperate. She just wanted to get out. Only her reluctance to seem like a coward kept her going.

Alas, she would never leave the forest alive.

She didn't know that Jai, the boy she was so eager to meet, lingered at their meeting point long past the decided hour but when he could wait no more, he turned back. Unaware that he had left, Nia wandered further into the heavily wooded area of the forest than she should have. Her enthusiasm was long gone, influenced greatly by the fading light. She felt a sinister vibe springing at her from every corner. The thorns pulling at her clothes and the branches grasping at wisps of her hair felt like monsters trying to grab her. Then came the crashing in the undergrowth behind her. It broke through the silence of the forest, startling her, propelling her to start running.

Ava tried to grab the girl's velvet cloak. She failed. The velvety softness brushed against her fingertips as if in silent mockery of her frantic attempt. The shadows ensnared Nia, making her invisible to Ava. Ava's sense of dread spiraled. What was about to happen? She didn't have to wait long for her answer. The thin unearthly scream that resounded through the forest left no doubt of the girl's fate.

A shriek made its way to Ava's lips. She suppressed it. She wanted to run in the opposite direction. Instead, she steeled herself. From her vantage point, behind a cluster of gnarled old trees with branches spread out the like the arms of an old crone, she combed the expanse nearby.

Ava had been pulled to the future before. The world was full of one calamity or another. Time travel drained her magical prowess, weakened her. If her future were to be filled with traumatic and foreboding events such as this one, then she would beg Siobhan, the queen of the Heichi sorceresses, to take her power away. It was impossible to look at death in the face and remain an observer. Her heart was beating so loudly. She was sure that anyone camouflaged by the darkness, man or creature, could use it as a beacon to uncover her hiding place.

Stay silent, stay hidden, and never let the ones you watch spot you, Ava repeated the mantra in her head again and again. Maybe the litany would act as a talisman against the impending disaster. She was barely able to hold it together. Trouble was in the air and she was right in the middle of it.

Things were about to get much worse.

Suddenly her searching eyes found the girl. Something was off, though. Earlier even scared to death, the girl had been full of life. Now her movements were lackluster and disoriented. She lurched and staggered; her ermine lined velvet cloak hanging at a crazy angle from her shoulder. Then the beautiful red cloak fluttered to the ground, making a garish contrast with the green and brown shell of the forest floor. As Ava watched, the light was just enough for her to see splashes of blood drip down from the girl's body and onto the earth below her feet. She was badly hurt. How? Why? The skin of her torso had been shredded to ribbons by vicious slashes. Ava stared in shock. Who did this to her? Ava debated breaking the rules. She was ready to take the risk. Ready to use magic to save the girl. The punishment would be terrible but she had to save her.

Ava almost stepped out from behind her hiding place, but at the same moment, the girl fell to the ground, a look of utter astonishment overshadowing her beautiful face. *She can't believe it's over,* thought Ava. As the life poured out of the girl, the terror in her eyes was replaced with a desolate vacuum. Before this, the girl had a life. Now she had nothing, except death. She had been through so much. As if in acknowledgement of her suffering, nature lent her dignity. Her cloak fluttered in the wind and its billowing folds draped themselves over her inert body like a shroud.

THE PROPHECY IS SET INTO MOTION - CAITLIN'S CHOICE

One fine autumn morning, Caitlin awoke in cold sweat. An ominous feeling besieged her. She hoped that it was temporary and would pass in the brightness of the day. But even as she watched the leaves fall from the trees, the words of the Wraith came back to haunt her. This time she could not shut them out.

Elbows on the table, her face cupped between her hands, Caitlin stared at her innocent children.

Michael saw her and said, "We are blessed. The two of them ask for nothing as long as they have each other."

She gave him a forlorn smile but time she could not bring herself to confide in him. He would think she was paranoid.

But she knew the truth. It burned and sizzled in her gut. Her past was no longer a threat far beyond the horizon. It was a dark hovering cloud. If anything happened to her family, she would never be able to forgive herself.

Obsessed by the prophecy, Caitlin began to fret.

"What ails you?" Michael asked again and again but she refused to confide in him. What would she tell him? What would he do? She never should have followed her heart. Love had made her weak and unable to make the sacrifice of walking away from Michael, but now… now it was time to put her family's welfare before her own selfish needs.

Caitlin finally saw a way out of her torment. She was born a guardian and it was now time to don that mantle again. She had to protect her little family. She and the cursed child must be separated from each other. If they were not together, the prophecy could not come to pass.

But how does a mother choose? Choosing between her children seemed implausible and unthinkable, but for the sake of her family, she had to do it. She had to know which child lived under the shadow of the curse.

In little Joshua, who was so innocent and without guile, Caitlin saw Michael and the peace and calm he brought to her life. In Talia, she saw an image of herself, the strength, the promise of power, and unfortunately, the pain it could bring. Talia was the half-blood, the prophecy predicting Caitlin would betray the Heichi on account of her child had to be related to Talia.

The blood of the Heichi flowed in Talia's veins, which meant she must be strong. Caitlin had seen glimpses of her daughter's power often enough, even if Talia didn't know her own strength. Joshua, on the other hand, was mortal. He needed his mother's magic. Caitlin knew that when that Talia was strong and when the time came Talia's powers wouldn't let her down.

After dwelling on her decision and changing her mind a thousand times, Caitlin hastily bundled up Joshua one night and fled.

"Where are we going?" a sleepy Joshua asked. "Is Talia coming too?"

"Go back to sleep, my little one," Caitlin pleaded as she snuck away. She left no note, no message. Separating herself from Talia to protect them all, Caitlin's intentions were noble. She knew there could be no long drawn goodbyes else her courage would fail her.

The next morning, Talia and Michael awoke to a world without Caitlin and Joshua. "Where are they?" a distraught Talia asked her father who was running his hands through his hair, his eyes darting from one corner to the other.

It was as if they had never existed. Any reminder of them had been ruthlessly destroyed or hidden by Caitlin. With her cowardice, Caitlin thus set into motion that which she had fought tooth and nail to avoid. She broke Michael's heart, inadvertently setting the prophecy in motion.

Talia and Michael took this blow differently. Michael was stoic for a few days. "They will return," he insisted, rubbing his hands together. "She is upset about something. She will return as soon as she calms down." But as days passed the hope in his eyes dimmed. He had always believed that their love would overcome Caitlin's fears, but he hadn't accounted for a mother's anxiety for her children or a wife's love for her husband. Caitlin genuinely believed that she was protecting them all by running away. As time went by with no sign of Caitlin or Joshua, Michael got frantic when he realized they were not coming back.

Talia's reaction had been more realistic. She ventured as far as she could without worrying Michael, making enquires to strangers: *"Has anyone seen a woman and a small boy?"* Sheer waiting would have driven her mad.

For a long time, Talia convinced herself that her mother and Joshua would return in their own time. But slowly the truth dawned. They were not coming back. She needed something to hold on to, a talisman to say good-bye. So, she turned the house upside down until she found one last toy of Joshua's that had escaped Caitlin's harsh de-cluttering. It was a clay horse. Clutching the little toy in her hands, Talia locked herself in her room, weeping buckets for days and nights until she had no more tears to shed.

When Talia finally emerged, she was no longer a child but the woman of the house. She had a father to care for and a household to manage. The innocent child of a few days earlier was gone forever. "No one has taken them, forcibly. Somebody would have seen something. Mother just does not intend to be found," she said, ice in her voice. "The two of us have to go on. I won't let you give up."

Excerpt from Metamorphosis

MIRACLES

Amelia

Liam found his answer in Zoe, a seasoned businesswoman and her ambitious venture, 'Miracles,' a crisis management and image-building firm. She had an admirable success ratio. Zoe would repackage a sinner as a saint or vice versa— tarnishing honest and upright reputations on demand to help her clients. If there was a black book for criminals, she probably figured in PR 101. Her agency worked with black hearts like Liam, making distasteful dealings disappear, and helping crooks like him get clean chits. It wouldn't be wrong to call her a fairy godmother to the villains. Of course, it all depended on the size of their wallets. With the sale of his diamonds on the wane, Liam wasn't flush with funds, but Zoe still jumped on board.

"I want to be known as a benevolent and an honest businessman," he said to Zoe.

A little too much, a little too late, I thought as Zoe's brows drew closer.

Zoe quickly reassured him when she noticed the beginning of a frown etched Liam's features because of her prolonged silence. "That's why I am here." She studied Liam in his well-fitted suit, silk tie, white shirt, and his Ivy League haircut. "You'd do beautifully"—she raised a hand as he began to grin jubilantly—"but there's been too much bad press about you. Besides, it's women who covet pink diamonds, so you're hardly the right choice to promote them."

"So, find an international face."

"The right ones for this delicate project will charge you through the nose, and you're barely able to pay me for *my* services." She smiled charmingly. "Also, you are bad news right now. No one worth their salt wants to be associated with Peradora or you."

Liam's eyes turned flinty, but Zoe barely glanced at him.

I marveled at her candor, wishing I had half her pluck.

Zoe waved her hand delicately. "We'll find a new face and build her up. Let's go local."

"Local?" Liam stared at her with raised eyebrows.

"I've heard Peradorian girls are beautiful. Let's put that to the test, shall we?"

Liam finally introduced me to Zoe later that evening. I smiled politely taking in her carefully styled corn-silk colored hair, ivory-satin shirt, and expensive beige, virgin-wool jacket. Sitting across the table from her differed significantly from peeping and eavesdropping from afar. I felt uncomfortable and clumsy before her grace and sophistication.

I thought she'd look through me and concentrate on Liam, but to his utter annoyance, she ignored him and stared at me throughout dinner, as my food grew colder, and I fiddled in my chair. She did not to talk to me, other than dinner small talk such as 'Please pass the cassava bread' and, 'What is this called? I must have the recipe,' pointing at the coconut choka.

Just when dessert was served, she said to Liam, clapping her hands together, her attractive smile posed and asymmetrical, exposing lots of teeth, "I've found the face of the Peradorian diamonds! Congratulations!"

Liam's fork clattered onto his plate. I knew he enjoyed his dessert, especially the custard blocks and conkies. He looked exasperated. *Where?* I wondered. *Her plane arrived only a few hours ago. Did she find some goddess-like creature at the airport?* Another thought occurred to me. *Could it be one of the maids?*

Liam was having the same problem as me. "Who is it?"

he asked, furrowing his brow as he glanced around as though expecting to see this paragon appear out of thin air.

Next, he will look under the table, I thought, stifling a giggle behind my fist.

"Right here." Zoe pointed at me. "And I didn't have to take a single step outside the mansion. Imagine the money I've saved you."

My laughter dissolved. *What was Zoe talking about? Why was she looking at me like that? Like a spider looking at a fly trapped in its web.*

Liam laughed. When Zoe didn't join in and continued staring at him pointedly, he stopped, clearing his throat. "You're serious?" he scoffed, as I knew he would. I didn't blame him. Zoe's suggestion was ludicrous. "My niece! She has no sense of fashion or personality and is as timid as a mouse."

You don't have to be so honest. Do you? I wanted to disappear. He was talking about me as if I wasn't there, and although Liam made a habit of trampling my self-confidence, it didn't mean I was used to it.

"Have you *seen* her?" Zoe sounded incredulous. "I mean, *really* seen her? She is gorgeous. Look at that cascading dark hair! Imagine if it was styled and layered. Her upturned blue eyes are lovely, and those long lashes! With the right make-up, they would be perfect for hypnotizing both men and women into buying your diamonds. Give me a chance. Let me work with her."

Hypnotize. People. Into buying diamonds. Me! The lady was loco.

Liam pressed his lips together, and tapped his fingers on the dining table. He was seconds away from throwing a fit. "There are plenty of pretty girls in Peradora, I am sure."

Zoe shook her head.

But he persisted. "You must find one. Anyone but her. She won't do."

Yes, uncle. Show her she is talking rubbish.

"She is the only one who will do," said Zoe. "She is related to you. She is family yet is untouched by the scandal swirling around you. I will position her as the 'Diamond Princess.'" Her tone grew enthusiastic as she looked at me calculatingly. "Her name will carry more weight than other girls. She is anything but ordinary. I know what I am doing. Trust me. You hired me. Say yes, and let me do my job."

Liam studied me carefully, a slow smile widening his lips, and I knew my future had been decided. It didn't matter that I was a wallflower, dreaded fuss, and the limelight, and hated the diamonds. This problem was one of my own design and I had been chosen to put out the fire that I had set. The irony of the situation made me want to weep and scream in frustration. Of course, I did none of that. I sat there, my lips set in a plastic smile, hands on my lap, as I shredded a paper napkin to bits under the table.

Things moved quickly after that, and I decided I had two choices. I could either grind my teeth, brace myself, wait for whatever was coming or sit back and enjoy the ride. I went with the latter.

Zoe took me to places I'd learned about, read about, and watched on television but had never been to—Paris, London, Amsterdam, and the States. We wandered into these vast stores on streets like Avenue Montaigne and Rue Saint Honoré, Oxford Street, Fifth Avenue, SoHo, and Broadway and picked up gorgeous designer dresses for me to wear. There was no sightseeing. Zoe was a woman with an agenda. It was an endless blur of preppy model types or older women with sleek hairstyles and well-cut suits who helped me in and out of clothes. The prices made me swoon, but Zoe didn't bat an eyelash. If Liam knew she was spending money like water, he'd probably self-combust. But I enjoyed myself, away from my golden cage, determined to make the most of my fleeting liberty.

I didn't care about the dresses. Or the shoes. Though, I had to admit, they were exquisite. What I loved was the freedom—the feeling that I had escaped my golden prison, however fleeting it was. The air smelled different. The people looked different. So unburdened, busy, and lost in their thoughts. They didn't constantly look around as though expecting to be thrown into prison at any moment. They said what they wanted, ate what they wanted, and worked the hours they wanted, choosing jobs they liked. They were so free; I envied them and felt sorry for them. They didn't know what they had. They didn't value it enough. Freedom to be your own person was precious, and these people were squandering it without realizing what they had. They didn't stop every hour, get down on their knees, and thank God. Perhaps that was the true value of their freedom—the luxury of taking it all for granted.

Not me. I was thankful for every minute away from Peradora and dreaded the day I would have to return.

A BESTIE FOR ME

The minute I crossed the threshold of Palacio my breathing became labored, and I felt my heart thumping wildly in my chest. The sense of freedom I'd embraced the past weeks flitted away as if it had never existed in the first place and I felt the old constraints fall into place.

But things were better than I expected.

"Someone is here to meet you," Zoe said. "A friend. Amelia, meet Theresa."

"A friend?" I blinked.

A young girl close to my age smiled tentatively at me. The first detail I noticed about her was her bangs, cut straight across her forehead, almost hiding her almond-shaped eyes. The rest of her brown hair fell loosely around her shoulders. She was quite tall and slightly hunched as if she hoped to blend into the background, while also angular and lean. She wore a black, cotton, polka-dotted skirt that fell somewhat above her knees and a white shirt tied in a knot at her waist. She stood there awkwardly, fidgeting with her hands.

I smiled at her reassuringly. *Like me. Like me.* The thought resonated in my head. Her smile grew wider. My eyes shone, and my heart burst with happiness. To a person who lived a life rich with love and friendship, my joy at the possibility of having a friend would appear pathetic. But my life was a lonely one. Citing safety reasons, my uncle had kept out of school and hadn't allowed me to mix with any local children or teenagers until today.

"My uncle gave you permission?" I asked Zoe, wide-eyed.

"Bah! I'm not scared of your uncle. He can learn to deal with a few changes. If you're going to be 'The Diamond Princess of Peradora,' you will need all the help you can get. I won't always be here."

"Zoe, you are leaving?" I asked, a feeling of dread enveloping me.

"Not right now. But soon. This is not my life. I have other clients too, you know."

Seeing my crestfallen face, she quickly added, "Of course, I'm very fond of you. You're much more than a client. And I will visit."

"Why didn't you tell me?"

"I'm telling you now, aren't I? That's why Theresa is here. When I leave, you won't be alone."

I hugged Zoe gratefully and whispered, "Thank you."

Then doubt clouded my features again. "Will *he* allow her to stay once you're gone?"

"What's the name of my firm?"

"Miracles," I said frowning.

"There is a reason for that, my girl. That's what I do. This girl isn't going anywhere. She is here to stay."

I thought Theresa would be a bit like me. Eager to stay out of Liam's way, but she surprised me. She never hovered nervously in his presence, never flinched when he was around. She spoke respectfully but not deferentially. Surprisingly it didn't bother Liam too much.

We did everything together. We went on long walks and chatted about this and that. We sat in the garden swinging our legs as we watched Liam's men go by. We ate tons of pizza, corn cakes, chicken taquitos, and munched on plantain chips. We guzzled glasses of champus, a refreshing pineapple drink, and terere, an ice-cold yerba mate tea, when the heat zapped us. Theresa loved ice cream. She could devour pints of it, perhaps a gallon. I never touched the stuff. I hated it. I broke out into a cold sweat the moment I caught sight of ice cream.

"You don't know what you're missing," Theresa said, at dinner one day. "Try some." She pointed at a bowl of rose-petal ice cream layered with nuts and chocolate chips. She stared at me in shock. "Why has your face turned green? Are you sick?"

"Leave her alone," Liam commanded. We hadn't noticed

him standing by the door. His eyes were filled with an under-standing I never expected. He remembered. "Are you okay?"

I quickly nodded and left the table, leaving a baffled Theresa behind. His unexpected kindness brought tears to my eyes. As for Theresa, she never mentioned ice cream again.

Zoe, I noticed, was going easy on me. I assumed she didn't want to spook me by rushing me into things, which allowed me time to slack off. But the trials of outfits and diamond jewelry soon began. We were about to be thrown right into the thick of things. Seeing the awe in Theresa's eyes when I dressed up made my heart swell. It made my hatred for the pink diamonds a little more bearable.

One day, when I was trying on an outfit, Theresa's hand repeatedly slid over a slinky gray dress lying on the lavender and white settee. It had a printed design a with a long V-neck, cuff-embellished raglan sleeves, and a slightly flared skirt. "Go on, try it," I said, nudging her lightly.

"You think it's okay?" Her eyes shone.

"Of course." I grinned. "Why shouldn't it be?"

That's when Zoe entered the room. "Take your hands off that dress," she shouted. "It's silk chiffon, you fool!"

The dress slid from Theresa's hands and almost fell on the floor. I grabbed it in time. "But … I told her she could try it on," I protested.

"What happens if Liam comes to know that the hired help

is trying on the clothes he spent big bucks on?" Zoe said, hands on her hips.

"She's my friend."

"That may be, but foremost, she works for you." Zoe glared at the two of us. "Neither of you forget that again, please."

"But you said she was a friend. Friends share." I jutted my chin.

"You're Amelia Diaz." Zoe sneered. "No one can truly be your friend. Your uncle is the dictator of this country." She pointed at Theresa. "All these little people are afraid of you. One word from you and her entire family can disappear. You still think she's your friend?"

"I would never do that. Theresa knows that," I said. "Theresa, you know that, right?" I asked.

Theresa's face turned red. She nodded stiffly.

"Is there going to be a problem?" Zoe asked, her shrewd eyes catching the anger simmering below Theresa's surface.

"No!" Theresa said. "I will be careful in the future, Señora."

As I rushed to apologize, Theresa shrugged my hand off and turned to look at me with a polite smile, a shuttered look in her eyes. "Don't," she said. "Whatever you say will only make things worse. Please let me do my job."

I was sorry—really sorry. But I didn't understand the full extent of Theresa's humiliation. A few days later, I cast the incident from my mind, but Theresa didn't. I continued to look at her as a good friend but failed to notice the coldness that she masked with a pretty smile and false cheer, and how her smile felt plastic from time to time. I didn't see how her eyes enviously followed me while I tried on the endless supply of clothes. How her fingers lovingly caressed the pink diamond bracelets, earrings, and necklaces I wore for the promotional photos. I never noticed because I thought she was my friend. I thought she enjoyed my company. The diamonds and clothes meant nothing to me, so I assumed it was the same for her. I did not see the truth then. My desperate longing for a friend blinded me to Theresa's hostility, which she masked with a veneer of friendliness.

Theresa hid her innermost thoughts and desires from me, and I wouldn't find out until much later how envy can turn into hate, and resentment into a desire for revenge.

The only thing Theresa was truly earnest and genuine about was her elder brother, Adrian. She glowed when she spoke about her wild, adventurous brother who she adored. She was critical of all the guys in the compound and spent hours listing their shortcomings compared to her brother. I good-naturedly listened when she boasted about him, peppering her with questions, but heart of hearts, I couldn't help envying their bond. She shared incredible tales about her brother's exploits, and I, who lived a sober, boring life, almost swooned in disbelief. There were times I laughed till tears leaked from my eyes.

"Adrian will visit me one of these days," she said confidently. "He will find a way. I'm his precious, one and only sister. Just wait and see."

I never really believed her. Who would dare defy Liam? No one. Not if they valued their freedom and maybe even their lives. "You're kidding, right? The guards will throw him in prison."

She grinned. "Scaling high walls hasn't been a problem for Adrian, since he was seven. It was only the climbing down that he mastered after turning nine."

"Who helped him down until then?" I asked, smiling.

Theresa clammed up, her face turning pale. She never answered my question, but the grief and heartache I saw told me there was a painful secret behind her silence.

The more she spoke about her family, the more I longed to meet them, especially the elusive Adrian. Her words conjured up the image of a dashing hero who rushed from one grand adventure to another, a strong, indestructible champion Liam would never be able to bully. I saw Adrian as an antithesis to my weak self and began building him up more and more in my imagination.

Can one adore someone without even meeting them? Maybe such is the silliness of young love. First love. Absurd. Unexplained. Illogical. It was my secret, and I guarded it closely, hoping against hope that one day I would meet my prince.

I was stuck in a dream world of my making, oblivious to what occurred around me. The heady combo of Theresa's friendship and thoughts of Adrian, a boy I hadn't even met, lulled me into an I-don't-have-a-care-in-the-world zone. My life was about to implode. I was on the crux of becoming famous. My next cage awaited, even if it was another golden one. But I didn't care.

The fake persona Liam, Zoe, and Theresa painstakingly wove for me was showcased to the world through social media. What do you do when you desire people to forget? You dangle gossip-worthy news before them. And that's precisely what Zoe did. She gave the people an alternative narrative. Me! I was promoted as the exotic new find from Peradora—'The Diamond Princess.'

Glamorous pictures of me appeared on all the significant gossip sites. The discreet pink diamond jewelry used in the shots was subtle but hard to miss. They added exactly the right touch of elegance and glamor to the outfits. My minders did such a great job that editors of fashion magazines and designers started seeking me out. And wherever I went, so did the diamonds, of course. Zoe's strategy was working.

My popularity skyrocketed, and the demand for the pink diamonds increased with it. People forgot the 'blood' diamond tag. Diamonds have always been a girl's best friend, but suddenly, rich girls all over the world were willing to give an arm and a leg—preferably someone else's—so they could own a pink diamond in any form; pendant, necklace, tiara, bracelet or best of all, an exotic out-of-the-world-expensive solitaire. I was aware they sought to emulate the diamond heiress of Peradora, not me, the real me. Peradora regained its place on the world map, more prominent and legitimate than before. Thanks to the primped, preened, and airbrushed version of me.

I realized that by allowing myself to be a part of this deception, I, too, would have the blood of countless innocents on my hands. I was now a part of Liam's regime. I wanted to speak up. I wanted to shout out against the diamonds and Liam. After all I had an international platform. But I stayed quiet, feeling every bit like the coward I was. As long as Liam could harm Abuelita I knew I couldn't; I wouldn't say a word.

The mines were up and running once again. I had only myself to blame.

I barely saw Zoe now; her work with us was done. I'd started traveling for fashion shows and events with the sole company of Theresa. Of course, an entourage of guards always accompanied us. Since they followed the rule of 'seen but not heard,' I had nothing much to say to them, nor they to me.

I perfected the 'it girl' look. I was the one who girls from all over the world adored and aspired to imitate, but I hated it all. People stared at me wherever I went. I acted like I didn't care, though their scrutiny bothered me. The fashion world had its own rules, written *and* unwritten. They wanted me to fall in line, become a marionette and do what the fashion gurus dictated. I wasn't supposed to express my opinion. They wanted an icon, not a thinker.

This world aspirational for so many was not without its flaws. One needed to remove their blinders to see reality. The glamorous life they had thrust me into differed from an insider's point of view. Backstage at a fashion show in Paris, I saw a too-thin model wearing a dress that was so tight she had to be cut out of it—leaving a frustrated designer in her wake. Let's not forget the combination of weird hairdos at the MET gala—more appropriate on tribal chiefs—and absurd dresses with trains, three miles long. I should know I tripped over one. At the Oscars, a beautiful actress, I admired fell flat on her face because of her oversized heels, while another was not allowed entry into a fundraising event because she wasn't wearing the right shoes. What did her shoes have to do with charity? The contrasts in this world made my head spin.

Most people of my acquaintance had short attention spans and little depth. Like magpies, they moved from one shiny new gossip to the next. They loved the sound of their own voices. All they needed from me were the 'oohs' and 'aahs' in all the right places. They didn't care if I listened as long as they had an audience to share their little tussles and battles with.

Fame wasn't all rainbows and sunshine. I was called a fraud; sometimes people called me the 'Ice Princess.' I tried taking the disparaging comments in stride, tried not to be affected by the vile words and the negativity. I couldn't do anything to change their thinking. The least I could do was acknowledge them, the good, the bad, and the ugly.

But any publicity is good. What started as a trickle of followers soon became a downpour. I was an unqualified success.

In my eyes, I had failed.

Excerpt of Redemption

Noah

The town of Oaxaca—the warehouse district, Mexico

The lethal jumble of sweat, blood, and leather told Noah that the Werexols shadowing him used the cover of darkness to get closer than he realized. His instincts in human form were not top-notch, and there was nothing he could do about it. He wasn't afraid, just a little wary and weary of the whole song-and-dance of the chase. He'd veered into an alley, thinking of skirting them but found himself facing a dead-end. Since he'd left Peradora, he'd hoped to be left alone, but heart-of-heart, he knew bad luck always found him. It was his constant friend. Now, at least, the wait was over.

He hoped to avoid violence, but how things went

depended on the Werexols. If they were in hunting mode, he would have no choice but to let Tagasaya take over. His inner monster was just below the surface, waiting and watching. He tasted battle in Peradora and now was baying for blood. Yielding to Tagasaya was the last thing Noah wanted. The memory of the skirmish with Liam's men made him feel nauseous. He had cut, torn through, and broken them as though they were nothing. He pushed the memories away and suppressed the bloodlust clawing at him. *If only I could avoid this fight.* He knew it wasn't going to happen, though. The relentless growling of the Werexols made it clear that they wouldn't concede without a fight.

Do they know I'm a predator, too?

A nonchalant female voice whispered in his head—*they have been told you're human.*

The voice was gone in a heartbeat. He thought he must have imagined it but listened carefully, just the same. There was nothing, just the thrum of his breathing and the quiet threat of his waiting attackers. He dwelt on the Werexols once more as he debated how to deal with them. He reflected, *when I was a toddler, I had a few older and tougher Werexol friends who protected me from supernatural bullies.*

As if she couldn't help herself, the bubbly voice spoke again. *But these guys aren't your friends. If you are a stranger to the werewolves, or they are ravenous, self-control is out of the question. The urge to kill overpowers them. Overtaken by blood lust, only their victim's death will satiate them. To make things worse, they rarely remember their murderous actions. This isn't a friendly Brady bunch. Beware!*

"Don't advise me," he snapped, clutching his head. "I don't even know who you are. Show yourself or get out of my head."

His flare-up didn't seem to ruffle the blatant intruder. She continued in the same unflappable tone. *I wanted to see how receptive you were to making a new friend. I thought it would be rude just to show up.*

"And jumping inside my head? That's not rude?" he growled. "I don't need friends. I'm fine alone. Show yourself or shut up. I'm not in the habit of talking to voices in my head."

A girl appeared by his side, making him jump. "Here I am, Tagasaya!" she said, giving him a bow with a flourish.

Noah's mouth fell open.

"Don't call me that," he said in an angry whisper. "How do you know my name? Why were you in my head? Why are you here now? Can't you see—"

"Shhh! Questions. Questions," she said, dropping the hood from her head.

The voluminous blue curls spilling over her shoulders, almost to her waist, drove his planned interrogation from his mind. A memory he had buried deep within the anvils of his mind burned behind his eyes. He could no longer see the girl. Instead, he saw—*a group of blue-haired women who stared at him with judgment and hatred in their eyes. His mother pleaded for his life, but they remained stony-faced, throwing him vile looks.* His precious mother had been a blue-haired sorceress—one of them. She called them 'sisters,' but they showed her no mercy and treated her like an outcaste.

Hate spilled through his veins. He wanted to unleash Tagasaya on the girl. *Stop*, said the voice in his head. *You're no monster. I was not one of the women who judged your mother.*

He stepped away from her, not trusting himself, not trusting Tagasaya. "What do you want?" he said through gritted teeth, his eyes on the Werexols, who were fast approaching. "Speak up. I don't have the time for this."

"Why, I'm here to help, Tagasaya," she said with a bright smile. "I'm Katie."

"I don't care who you are. I know what you are. And I don't need help from the likes of you. I've experienced first-hand how helpful you lot can be."

"How very polite and welcoming you are!" the girl exclaimed sarcastically.

He glared at her. "I prefer to be called Noah," he said, even as he shifted into a defensive stance.

"Call yourself whatever you want. Take on any form you want, but don't forget who you really are."

There was no mockery in her voice. She spoke as though she'd known him for years. As though he was no stranger to her, and his bitter reality didn't faze her.

"You have spent most of your life denying the truth. You are as much Tagasaya as you are Noah."

"He is a monster," he said. "How do I accept him as a part of me?"

"Did he save the girl you sought to protect?"

"He did," Noah admitted.

"Then he is what you make of him."

Her words stunned him. He never thought of it quite that way.

"I am Heichi, but I promise I mean you no harm. Ask the werewolves what they want. Let's deal with this situation, and then we will talk," she said, drawing him out of his contemplation.

I won't take orders.

Fine. Then wait for the werewolves to attack.

"Werexols," he corrected her. "Humans call them werewolves. And you are not human."

Her face broke into an incredulous grin. "From all appearances, they're here to attack you, not toast a long and continued friendship, and you're wasting time arguing about what to call them? I call them 'werewolves' because I've lived among humans for a long time, even if I'm not one. I've adapted to a lot of their ways."

Her words resonated. He, too, had spent most of his life amid humans. Shaking his head, Noah tried to ignore the memories. He didn't want to empathize with her. He merely wanted to understand her motives. Empathy stimulated weakness. He had to seal away his emotions if he needed to soldier on. It wouldn't do him any good to learn more than necessary. He didn't want to find common ground. He only wanted the truth. It was best to stick to the basics.

"Did you lead them to me?"

"Obviously not." She raised her eyebrows. "My, what a wild imagination you have." One hand on her hip, she threw him an impish smile. "Didn't I say you could trust me?"

He snorted. "Doesn't mean I have to believe you." He pointed toward the Werexols. "They're here, and so are you. Too much of a coincidence, if you ask me."

She shook her head, making a show of being affected by his harsh words. Noah glared at the sorceress, smirking. *It's all an act. But you won't fool me. I watched as your queen manipulated my mother toward her death. How can I forget that? How can I trust any of you, no matter what you say?*

"I'm not asking you." Now both hands were on her hips.

She gave off the 'bossy' vibe perfectly, but rather than being fazed, he was only irritated.

"I'm informing you I'm here to help. And for your information I'm not bossy."

"I. Don't. Need. Help," Noah ground out. "Not from the likes of you. How many times do I need to tell you?"

She recoiled at the venom in his voice. "You can't be Selena's son. I heard she was thoughtful and kind. You're nothing like her."

"Yeah? And what did she get in return? So, please forgive me if I come across as less than perfect. I might make a horrible 'human being.' But I mostly get the job done alone." He wagged a finger at her and then held it to his lips. "Don't mention my mother's name. You don't want me getting mad at you."

"As if you could hurt me." She tossed her hair over her shoulder. Her tone softened. "And Selena was a fellow sister, so I'm free to talk about her."

Noah's shoulders tensed. "Selena was *my* mother, and she was banished by your queen. She wasn't your sister because she wasn't a sorceress anymore."

"I'm sorry." Her tone was contrite. "But this is important. You'll soon realize that you do need my help."

Noah had no shortage of enemies. Liam Diaz, the erstwhile dictator of Peradora, was a recently acquired dangerous adversary. As part of his now-defunct plan, Noah worked for Liam for a while, so he knew how vengeful Liam could be. This, though, was not Liam's signature behavior. If Liam caught up, a battalion of armed thugs, not Werexols, would surround Noah.

Supernatural hunters bore the hallmarks of—*Siobhan*. His fingers clenched into a fist. *Why can't she leave me alone?* In her eyes, he was an abomination—the love child of supernatural parents from different clans. He wanted to fade into oblivion, but she wouldn't allow it. She believed she was waging a holy war against him. He hid from her for years, right under her nose in Peradora. But now the Werexols, natural trackers among the supernaturals, had caught up with him.

It was time to get this over with.

"What do you want?" Noah asked as he nodded in the general direction of the Werexols who stood in the shadows. He'd deal with the sorceress later. From the corner of his eye, he saw her pull back a little as he spoke.

There was a quick huddle among them, and a Werexol, who had to be the pack-master, stepped forward. Long, matted, dark hair covered its disproportionately large, muscular torso and arms.

"Having a bad hair day?" Noah asked. He heard the sorceress gasp in shock. She wanted him to talk them down, not rile them further. That's precisely what he set out to do, but before he knew it, the words were out of his mouth.

The pack-master growled, its eyes blazing, and flexed its sharp claws. The combination of a scarred, bald-head, covered with tattoos and crazy eyes gave it an odd appearance.

"Hair, hair everywhere except on your head where it should be," Noah said.

"Shut up," the sorceress snapped from behind him. "What is the matter with you? Do you have a death wish?"

"Shut up," growled the pack-master.

"Ah! You speak." Noah grinned like an idiot. It was also a toss-up—which alarmed him more—the creature's pointed teeth or claws. Then there were the other Werexols, who stood in small groups behind the large one, further under-lining its position of authority.

"Who sent you?" Noah asked.

His question incited no response.

The sorceress gave an impatient huff. He ignored her. The leader persisted in scowling while low growling emerged from the remaining Werexols standing in the shadows.

He turned to the girl he had almost forgotten. "They're no kindergarten squirts, I know. They probably have enough blood on their hands—"

"Nevertheless, you don't want to hurt them," she finished for him.

"You're in my head again," he grumbled. "But, yes. Tagasaya's rage and bloodlust are not something I love. I don't particularly enjoy being a killer."

"That's expected," she said. "Despite being Dueijian, your father, Satoshi, was no killer, either."

"You knew him?"

"Knew of him," she corrected him. "A Dueijian who stole the heart of a Heichi sorceress must have been exceptional indeed."

Praise for the father, he only had fading memories of, made him beam at her. "So, what do we do about them?" He gestured toward the antsy Werexols.

"There is a way," she said.

"Spit it out. We don't have much time."

She bit her lip. "I bet it won't be your go-to solution."

He gave a mirthless laugh. "I don't care. I want out."

"We make a run for it."

"What?" He massaged the back of his neck as he

absorbed her suggestion. "A coward's way?" he finally spluttered.

"Or a prudent person," she corrected him, giving him a wink. "I told you, you wouldn't like it."

He rolled his eyes. "I don't have to like something to know it is a good idea. It is fight or flight. The Werexols are not open to reasoning, so flight it is."

* 9 7 9 8 8 9 5 5 6 8 4 8 4 *